"Evocative... Nam as it m̲...
—Ed Gorman, *Cedar Rapids* ...

"Got purple smoke at one o'clock!"

"Looks like the wind is coming right at us, so we'll just do a straight run-in." Hines dropped the helicopter to ten feet above the tall palms that marked the boundaries of the paddies. He lowered the collective to flatten the big blades and slow the craft to a halt over the purple smoke.

Huddled forms approached from the tree line, carrying a poncho on which a small man writhed in obvious pain. After a few moments Hines looked over his shoulder to see how the transfer of the wounded guy was coming. The pilot noted in surprise that the casualty was actually smiling!

Hines turned to his copilot and saw the men standing just outside the thinning purple smoke, the muzzles of their weapons a scant inch away from the Plexiglas. Icy fingers gripped his heart as he recognized the weapons, fingers that tightened all the more when he followed the various barrels back to the faces behind them.

They were smiling, too.

"Vietnam: Ground Zero... are books to linger in the mind long after their reading."
—*The Midwest Book Review*

Also available by Eric Helm:

VIETNAM: GROUND ZERO
P.O.W.
UNCONFIRMED KILL
THE FALL OF CAMP A-555
SOLDIER'S MEDAL
THE KIT CARSON SCOUT
THE HOBO WOODS
GUIDELINES
THE VILLE
INCIDENT AT PLEI SOI
TET
THE IRON TRIANGLE
RED DUST
HAMLET

VIETNAM: GROUND ZERO™

MOON CUSSER

ERIC HELM

A GOLD EAGLE BOOK FROM
WORLDWIDE®

TORONTO • NEW YORK • LONDON • PARIS
AMSTERDAM • STOCKHOLM • HAMBURG
ATHENS • MILAN • TOKYO • SYDNEY

A special thanks to TMC Roe E. Markin, Sr., USN (Ret.) and Major Bill Davis, U.S. Army Special Forces, for their support and encouragement.

First edition December 1988

ISBN 0-373-62715-7

Copyright © 1988 by Eric Helm.
Philippine copyright 1988. Australian copyright 1988.

All rights reserved. Except for use in any review, the reproduction or utilization of this work in whole or in part in any form by any electronic, mechanical or other means, now known or hereafter invented, including xerography, photocopying and recording, or in any information storage or retrieval system, is forbidden without the permission of the publisher, Worldwide Library, 225 Duncan Mill Road, Don Mills, Ontario, Canada M3B 3K9.

All the characters in this book have no existence outside the imagination of the author and have no relation whatsoever to anyone bearing the same name or names. They are not even distantly inspired by any individual known or unknown to the author, and all the incidents are pure invention.

® are Trademarks registered in the United States Patent and Trademark Office and in other countries. T.M. are Trademarks; registration applied for in the United States Patent and Trademark Office and in other countries.

Printed in U.S.A.

VIETNAM: GROUND ZERO™

MOON CUSSER

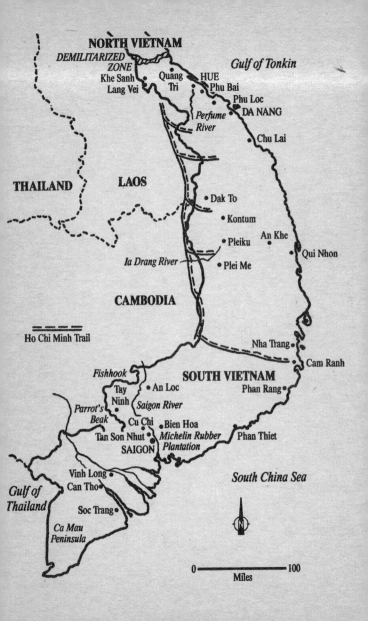

PROLOGUE

**MEKONG RIVER REGION
RVN**

The UH-1D rocked unsteadily onto the toes of its skids as the peta-prime of the pad released its sticky grip. U.S. Army Special Forces Captain MacKenzie K. Gerber instinctively covered his eyes with a hand to fend off flying debris, then turned to walk back toward the compound. The Huey rose to a hover, brown peta-prime icicles hanging from skids like crocodile teeth, then dipped its nose to run forward for take-off.

Gerber raised one hand from his face to return a farewell wave from the copilot and was rewarded with a gritty gust of rotor wash. He uttered a curse that was lost in the slap of retreating rotor blades. He cursed the heat, the sand in his eye and the sticky peta-prime the engineers insisted on spraying everywhere to keep down dust. He cursed the Army, the war and the pastel envelope he'd just received on the morning mail run.

Gerber was a young man, just over thirty, six feet tall with light brown hair and steely eyes. He'd already served one tour in Vietnam and was well into his second. He was a lean man, having dropped the little excess weight he'd picked up during his time in the World. Now he looked lean and mean.

The vagrant winds left by the helicopter were starting to die down around him when Gerber heard a change in the pitch of the retreating rotor blades. His eyes were seasoned by a year and a half of listening to and for helicopters, sometimes with his very life riding on their timely arrival, so he had no trouble spotting the craft in the distance. The change in tone was merely due to its turning crosswind. Gerber watched the chopper until it was an indistinct dot on the horizon that faded in and out of focus. He tried to pick it up again by looking off to one side, but found the rising sun there and lost the ship in a flash that caused him to squint.

While waiting for his vision to return, he wondered what it would be like to fly. The pilots seemed such a carefree bunch, all swagger and daring with a damned near wanton disregard for most regulations. Not so different from his own lot in life in those regards, he decided. The main difference was that they were up there where a cool breeze could be had just by cracking a window and climbing a few feet, while he was down here feeling the sweat run down his back and smelling—perfume?

He stared at the envelope again, turned it over in his hands, then started to shove it into the left shirt pocket of his jungle fatigues. As an afterthought he crammed it into the right pocket, the left being too close to his heart and perhaps symbolic somehow. There was so much on his mind just now, so much to think about, and he really didn't need the extra hassle.

Gerber's eyes scanned the horizon one last time and found it vacant. He started off toward the compound, listening to the drone of a fat fly orbiting his head, wondering what the helicopter guys would be thinking of about now.

WHAT THEY WERE THINKING of was holidays.

"Yeah, we used to always get new duds at Easter back home when I was a kid," the soon-to-be-nineteen copilot allowed.

Warrant Officer Derek Hines, the pilot, squelched a smirk at the new guy's reference to childhood, then reflected on the fact that he was only a year or so older himself. Childhood seemed farther back than that somehow.

"We did that, too. New clothes and shoes at Easter and more just before school started in the fall. I think that's why I never really cared that much for Easter, having to go with Mom to the shoe store and then sprucing up for church and all."

"Yeah, my mama was a big one for church on the holidays, too. Easter, Mother's Day, Thanksgiving, Christmas. Always church and food. Lots of food! Guess I'll miss all that this year, huh?"

Hines picked up on the mournful tone in his copilot's voice and wished he could think of something more reassuring to say. Wished, in fact, that he could remember the guy's name! Patterson? Peterson? He gave up and fell back on the ruse Southerners had used for years when names eluded them.

"Don't worry, Bubba. They feed pretty well over here on the holidays, and if you're lucky enough to still be flying ash-and-trash when they roll around, you'll be amazed at how popular you'll be when you deliver it to the field."

The copilot, whose name was actually Pederson, smiled a thin smile that died quickly. He shook a gray thought out of his mind and went back to the subject.

"Guess what I'll miss most about Thanksgiving is the smell of everything cooking and all the menfolk going rabbit hunting the morning before the feast."

"The rabbit hunting you probably won't miss much," Hines stated truthfully. After nearly a year in-country, he doubted he'd ever have the desire to hunt again. "I think what I missed most about last Thanksgiving was my mother's butt."

Pederson's mouth dropped open at this, causing Hines to laugh out loud before explaining.

"What I mean is, a *picture* of my mother's butt. You see, Dad's never been one for snapping a lot of photos on holidays. Matter of fact, back when he and Mom had a camera apiece, he once recorded three straight Christmases on the same roll of film! Anyway, one picture he never misses is when Mom pulls the turkey out of the oven. Every year, as regular as clockwork, there's a shot of Mom's butt sticking out of the oven. Over the years there's been progressively less turkey showing and more and more Mom, so I can just about tell you what year the picture was made just by the width of Mom's butt. I really missed that last year."

"And she just lets him take her picture that way? I mean, she don't say anything about it?"

"Sure! She raises mortal hell. That's what makes it so much fun! Dad sneaks around with his Instamatic so as to be in position when she goes for the bird, and then—"

"Dust-off, Dust-off, this is Avalon Two. I have an evac mission for you," came a disembodied voice over the UHF.

Pederson and Hines looked at each other briefly, then turned their attention back to the voice on the radio as it resumed.

"Dust-off, Dust-off, this is Avalon Two. I have a priority evac, over," it said in a calm voice.

Hines waited a short interval for Dust-off to reply and, when no answer came, keyed his floor mike.

"Avalon Two, this is Hornet Three-Five. Say your coordinates, situation and casualties and I'll try to relay for you."

"Thank you, Hornet. My position is grid echo-tango-two-four-three-four. We are not, repeat, not in contact. Casualty is snakebite, over."

Hines's finger followed the coordinates on his acetate-covered map, the finger coming to rest on a point south of Highway One and west of his home base at Cu Chi. The point was, in fact, less than ten klicks from his present position.

"Avalon Two, Hornet Three-Five again. I can pass your request to Dust-off and you should have a chopper in twenty mikes. Ask your medic if there's anything else I need to tell them."

After a pause of several seconds, the voice returned with its first noticeable emotion.

"Casualty *is* our medic! Tell Dust-off hurry! Over."

"Roger that. Understand medic is the casualty, wait one. Break-break, Hornet Ops, this is Three-Five. Are you copying any of this?"

A scratchy patch of static answered, followed by the garbled mess of whistles and gibberish that comes from several units trying to transmit at the same time. It was an all-too-common phenomenon in the South where radio discipline was lax to the point of often being nonexistent.

"Hornet Ops, Three-Five, you were stepped on. I say again, are you copying Dust-off request from Avalon Two?"

More static, whistles, and gobbledygook. Irritated now, Hines made a decision.

"Hornet Ops, Three-Five in the blind. I'm diverting to scarf a casualty at grid echo-tango-two-four-three-four. My ETA at the triage pad is two-zero mikes. Snakebite victim, I say again, snakebite. Break-break. Avalon, Hornet Three-Five's inbound to you. Estimate six mikes. Do you have smoke?"

"This is Avalon Two. Yes, we have smoke grenades."

"Roger, wait until you hear me and then pop it."

"Okay, will do!"

"I'll take it for a spell, Bubba," Hines said evenly, then wiggled the cyclic stick between his legs gently to signify he had control of the ship. "This should be a simple scarf, but you always want to let base know what you're up to. We had a guy, Thomas, stop to drop off some extra rations to some buds in the field once, a single-ship mission like this one, see? Anyway, he didn't check in first. He landed right slap in the middle of some comm wire the VC had strung and really assed up his rotor head, but that wasn't the worst of it. His buddy's radio got soaked in a canal crossing and had about the same range as a water pistol! Had to leave the ship where it was and walk out with the grunts the next day. Of course we mounted a full search for the chopper, which meant we had to dodge a few other missions, so our Six was pissed when they come dragging in. Made the whole crew sit alerts every night for a month!''

"I'll remember that," Pederson allowed, then went back to studying the crisscross system of canals sliding by beneath them.

"I'll start a climb here so we can pick up the smoke easier. Sometimes when you're working in thick jungle it takes a while for the smoke to work its way through the canopy, but out here it should stand out like a bloody nose on a polar bear," Hines said, then rechecked his position and began a gentle turn to the west.

"Got purple smoke at one o'clock," Jennings, the crew chief, declared over the ICS.

"Got it!" Pederson almost shouted, then pointed to where a plume of violet was beginning to rise from the base of a tree line a short distance away.

"Good eyeballs. Looks like the wind is coming right at us, so we'll just do a straight run-in. It's pretty mushy around here, so we'll want to check the surface before we set her down. Don't want to get stuck with the grunts like old Thomas did, do we?"

Pederson agreed with a shake of his head, then grimaced as another spate of excited garbage filled his helmet.

"Sounds like someone's got an open mike," he said.

"Probably Avalon. Sometimes these guys get so excited they never let go of the mike button. It gets worse during a fire-fight, of course. That was probably these guys calling their smoke. Just roger 'purple' and here we go."

As Pederson was making the confirmation, Hines dropped the helicopter until it was a scant ten feet off the random tall palms that marked the boundaries of the paddies. A short way out, he slid the ship to the right and dropped below the last trees to run toward the billowing smoke.

This was the kind of flying Hines enjoyed, near enough to the ground to get the sensation of speed yet near enough to friendly forces to not sweat ground fire. His touch was light on the controls, and the helicopter ungrudgingly did his bidding, much to the chagrin of the new pilot, who didn't have the benefit of Hines's hundreds of hours in the air. All but a few of those hours had been in-country, too, he reflected, and reasoned that having survived the past eleven months was justification enough to be proud of his abilities. And enough to justify showing off just a bit, too.

He reefed the ship back into a tail-standing flare while lowering the collective to flatten the big blades and slow the craft to a halt just over the purple smoke. Anticipating the helicopter in a way that truly impressed the junior pilot, he pulled in just enough pitch to ease the ship to the ground right atop the still-smoking grenade, then lowered the collective.

Huddled forms approached from the tree line, carrying, and at times almost dragging, a poncho on which a small man writhed in obvious pain. Indistinct though the men were through the purple haze, Hines could tell they were Vietnamese due to their stature and the way they stopped far lower than necessary while advancing under the rotor blade.

"Looks like someone else might make it home in time for Easter, huh, Bubba?" he said with a smile, then reached into his pocket and pulled out a flattened and somewhat soggy pack of Kools.

He fished a misshapened cigarette from the pack and clamped it between his teeth, then looked over his shoulder to see how the transfer of the wounded man was coming. No, he had to admit, what he really wanted to see was how bad the guy was swollen from the snakebite and where he'd been bitten. He'd heard the standard tale told to all new arrivals about the guy who was answering a call of Mother Nature along the trail and was bitten right on the tip of his dick by a banded krait. He also remembered with a grin what the medic allegedly said to the victim after considering the recommended first aid in such cases. He'd said, "You're gonna die!"

Hines made a mental note to pass this story on to the new guy, then noted that the casualty being loaded into his helicopter appeared to be in better shape than the man in the story. In fact, this victim was so healthy he was actually smiling! A remark about this inconsistency died on Hines's lips as he turned to his copilot and saw the men standing just outside the cockpit in the thinning purple smoke, the muzzles of their weapons a scant inch away from the Plexiglass. Icy fingers gripped his heart as he recognized the weapons, fingers that tightened all the more when he followed the various barrels back to the faces behind them.

They were smiling, too.

1

SPECIAL FORCES CAMP
A-555

"So? Think you'll have to buy a new hat this time in?" Master Sergeant Anthony B. Fetterman, U.S. Special Forces, inquired of his captain, then fought unsuccessfully to keep a grin in check. Fetterman was a diminutive man with black hair that was thinning, a heavy beard that required him to shave twice a day and the kind of face that looked as if it belonged to a door-to-door salesman. That was until you looked in the eyes. Then you knew that Fetterman was someone not to be crossed.

"Didn't say, Tony. Knowing Colonel Bates as we do, I doubt I'd get a summons to Saigon for anything as pedestrian as promotion to major. More likely he wants to chew on my ass a little more for losing that Air Force dude up north."

"Not your fault," Fetterman said with a grunt as he leaned forward to take the offered bottle from Gerber. "They chose him, right? Still wonder where he got off to, though."

Gerber watched with detached interest as the smaller man lifted the Beam's Choice to his lips with obvious reverence, then tilted his head back to allow a thin stream of the smooth liquid to run down his throat. The sun flashed off either the bottle or the master sergeant's thinning scalp, causing Gerber to blink. "Yeah, I wonder about that, too. With a night jump, he might have opened too soon and drifted off to God knows where. Probably sitting around counting knotholes in Hanoi by now."

Fetterman lowered the bottle and sat with eyes closed, savoring the whiskey. "Or maybe he fixated and never pulled. Could be he's buried ass-deep in a rice paddy and some North Vietnamese will have a bumper crop next year. That's not our province, Captain. Besides, if the colonel wanted some more of your hide, he'd have taken it during our debrief. More's the pity, though. For an officer, the man *does* chew ass rather well."

It was a compliment, Gerber knew. Chewing ass and shining shoes were two things every senior NCO worthy of his stripes prided himself in, and acknowledging a talent for either in an officer was high praise.

"Yeah, well, I've been on the receiving end of enough of them to grant him that much," the captain began while retrieving the bottle, then took a small swig and finished with, "Yet I'll bet I'll still have ass left when he's got false teeth!"

Laughter rattled around the inside of the small hootch as if glad to be free. Fetterman rose to leave, citing a need to check conditions on the striker side of the camp. Gerber wasn't certain but thought this might be a subtle hint.

"I'm heading that way in a few, Tony. Need to have some last-minute words with Captain Minh and Sergeant Krung before I go. Speaking of which, did you have a chance to speak with Krung?"

The master sergeant's eyes shifted to the floor for a moment. It was a sore subject. He'd have to rate Sergeant Krung as probably the best striker he'd ever fought beside, a man whose performance under fire rivaled that of any American. If anything, Krung was almost too efficient at killing, too dedicated. But it was what Krung did to the enemy *after* they were dead that the captain was referring to.

Earlier in the week, a theater-wide message had come down from General Abrams himself, citing Army policy on "desecration of enemy remains,'' which put Krung in a bad light. Apparently there had been a rash of American dead found with varying degrees of disfigurement, and the powers that be reasoned it was in retaliation for some souvenir taking on the part of U.S. forces. Ears were cited in particular, as were fingers. Sergeant Krung collected a far more sensitive part of the anatomy from his kills and had vowed to collect a minimum of fifty of them—ten for each member of his family the Vietcong had murdered.

"No, sir, I haven't. You know how he is about that. It makes perfect sense to him. More than that, it's justice, payback, all that.''

"I can't argue that, Tony. But it's an order. I got it. I've given it to you. Now you pass it on to Sergeant Krung most ricky-tick!''

"But—''

"But what?''

"But, sir, he's so damned *close*! The ten-for-one thing was an oath, a matter of honor. I doubt he'll keep doing it after the oath is fulfilled, and with a little luck he should have his board full before long.''

Gerber pulled on his web belt, wiggled his hips from side to side until it settled into its accustomed fit, then refastened it. A grim look came over his face, causing thin lines to crinkle at the corner of each eye as though he were staring into a distant sun. When he turned, his jaw was squared in a manner the master sergeant recognized as indicating decision. He wasn't all that sure that Krung would quit. Gerber knew he was fulfilling a promise to kill VC to avenge the death of Lieutenant Bao, having finished the task of avenging his family.

"How many more does he need?''

"Four, I think. Maybe six at the outside.''

"Talk to him, Master Sergeant. The Marines are slaying enemy hand over fist up in Khe Sanh, and all the papers can say is doom for our side. The chief of police shoots a Vietcong officer who's just murdered another policeman and his entire

family and it's front-page news around the world, identifying
the gook as a 'suspect.' The brass hats are jumping through
their collective asses right now over all the adverse publicity
we're getting here, and the last thing we need is some snoop
popping in here and finding Krung's collection of Cong cocks!
Understood?''

"Yes, sir, understood!''

"Good. Now let's go.''

The inspection tour took them along the perimeter of the
rebuilt Camp A-555 as they checked machine gun and mortar
emplacements, integrity of concertina wire and minefields and
the general material condition of entrenchments. After the
camp was closed and dismantled, it was discovered by the
brass hats in Saigon that it had been effective in interdicting
the supplies flooding into the South. Studying the situation,
they had moved it and then rebuilt it.

But like everything else in Vietnam, the various bunkers and
entrenchments bore close scrutiny in a country where the life-
span of a rifle sling was only three months and that of the average burlap sandbag less than two. The new rubberized
sandbags aided in maintaining solid bunkers and trenches, but
the unrelenting extremes of heat and humidity, monsoon and
drought, made for a never-ending battle between man and
nature.

Along the striker hootches they saw Sergeant Krung super-
vising the efforts of a work party. The Nung Tai warrior looked
every inch his reputation. Fetterman felt a twinge of dread
creep up his spine as his captain cleared his throat to speak,
assuming a confrontation with Krung was at hand, but it was
only a reminder to test-fire the mortars once their sandbags
were replaced.

Once satisfied the perimeter was up to snuff, the men moved
into the interior of the camp along the inner circle of hootches
and team shacks that surrounded the C-shaped redoubt. As
they neared the base of the fire control tower, the inspection

was interrupted by the hasty arrival of Sergeant Galvin Bocker, the team's overgrown senior communications specialist.

"Captain, your chopper just checked in about twenty mikes out, and there's some traffic from Cu Chi," Bocker stated, then offered Gerber written versions of the transmissions.

"Whose ship is it?" Gerber asked.

"Colonel Bates's, sir. I thought he was with the Tenth in Okinawa. Anyway, it seems they're anxious to see you up there."

"He's back here," Gerber said, "at least temporarily, and assigned to MACV-SOG." The Special Forces captain tried to decipher the rabid scrawl that was Bocker's handwriting. Pulling a frown, he gave up after several attempts that yielded him either a prescription for worm tablets or the Lord's Prayer in Sanskrit. "Honestly, Galvin. How the hell can you be such a genius with tiny little circuits and such yet write like you're wearing boxing gloves? I can't make this shit out. How about giving me the gist of it, and for God's sake, print from now on, okay?"

"Yes, sir," Bocker agreed, a hurt tone in his voice that would have seemed comical, given his advantage in height and weight over both his superiors, had it not been genuine. "As I said, your helicopter's inbound about twenty minutes east, but they may take a few to look for a downed aircraft. That's what the other message is about, sir. Cu Chi is doing a radio search for Hornet Thirty-five, which didn't make it back this morning. Since we were the last stop on their route, they wanted to know if the crew reported any mechanical problems or fuel shortage while they were here. I was just going to ask around."

The lines on Gerber's face tightened at this news, then released as he reached back into the mental compartment marked 'Helicopter, this morning' and tried to recall anything that might be helpful. There was nothing significant.

"No need to go further, Galvin. I met the ship myself and everything seemed to be hunky-dory with them. Chief Warrant Officer Hines was flying, and he had an FNG copilot along. They didn't put out a Mayday or anything?''

"No, sir. Seems they did try to check in a time or two, but Cu Chi only got their call sign before another transmitter stepped on them. According to Flash, their dispatcher, the calls didn't sound particularly urgent, just the standard 'I'm out here and will soon be there' sort of thing. Anyway, if they don't find wreckage or survivors before dark, they request we put a couple of squads in the field to hunt for them in the morning.''

"Master Sergeant?" Gerber said while trying to figure how the series of squiggles and squirms on Bocker's message pad could possibly relate to what he'd just heard.

"No problem that I see. Captain Minh's been anxious to get some of his new Vietnamese troops out for a walk, anyway, and it would be a good training opportunity. I could send Johnson with them and take Galvin here, Krung and some Tais out myself, so long as there's transport, of course.''

"Cu Chi's providing the lift," Bocker added helpfully, still a little sensitive about the attack on his penmanship.

"If Minh wants to take his boys out for a jaunt, let him, but I'd recommend keeping Anderson with the other squad since Minh has his own medics. Try to rotate the patrols so that either Minh or yourself remain in camp at all times, Master Sergeant. The exec is a good man, mind you, but he's still new and probably doesn't appreciate what we're dealing with here, having Nung Tais and lowland Vietnamese in the same camp. Might want to send Galvin here with the strikers now that I think about it. His writing may not be so hot, but at least he'll be understood over the radio, and you know how Corporal Nhoc comes across when he's excited.''

"Yes, sir," Fetterman said, remembering several times when the LLDB RTO's voice had reached up into soprano range while calling in air strikes and fire missions. Not that Nhoc was scared—far from it. He just got so excited about killing people and breaking things that his voice got away from him.

"Well, guess I'd better get back and throw a couple of things in a bag before the copter gets here. Get Hornet Ops on the horn and tell them we'll do what we can to help find their lost chick, and cite the master sergeant as their point of contact."

Bocker hurried back to the semicool shelter of his commo bunker while the others completed their rounds with a quick stop at the ammo bunker. After noting a few minor housekeeping items that the master sergeant dutifully wrote down for correction, Gerber realized he was merely delaying the inevitable. As he was about to take his leave and head to his hootch, Fetterman stopped him cold with a question.

"Are you going to read it, or do you want me to dispose of it for you?"

Gerber looked shocked at first, then smiled in wonder.

"How'd you know? Am I that flustered?"

"Nope, but I figured either you'd received a letter on this morning's chopper or you'd taken to wearing that delightful perfume yourself. I was just giving you the benefit of the doubt."

"Yeah, another one. Haven't decided yet about reading it, Tony. Don't really see any point to it. Not after everything else that has happened. I would have thought that leaving her in the World without any notice would have convinced her."

"Well, that's all up to you, of course, but if you're planning on seeing our favorite journalist while in Saigon, I'd recommend leaving it here. I get the feeling there's enough sibling rivalry between those two already."

"You're right about that, Tony, and about the letter, too. Want me to bring you anything back?"

"A case of beer might be nice. Anything except Black Label, if it's not too much trouble."

"You got it. See you in a couple of days, I hope. This didn't turn out to be much of a homecoming for me. I mean, here only two days, then right back to MACV-SOG. When Master

Sergeant Sload gets back to relieve you, we'll set aside a couple of days to unwind. Maybe have a good drunk, look up some old friends or something."

"Sounds good," Fetterman said seriously while reflecting that the Special Forces was hardly a business where friends were allowed to grow old. "Give my regards to the colonel."

"I'll do that, Tony, and in the meantime make damned sure I don't come back here to find the boys have been taking scalps."

FETTERMAN WAS SITTING in the team house with Sergeant First Class Derek Kepler having dinner, and a fine dinner it was, when the radio crackled its message. To the untrained eye, the meat would have appeared to be thick-cut Delmonico steaks, charcoal-broiled almost to a cinder and smothered with onions, but it wasn't. Instead, Tony Fetterman knew that somewhere in IV Corps there walked one less water buffalo. But the onions were genuine, and his trusty Case VS-21 knife found little resistance when slicing through the meat.

Fetterman enjoyed the change of pace, which meant he didn't question the meat's source. Early on he'd learned not to inquire too closely when SFC Kepler came into a windfall. It was much wiser just to dispose of the evidence as quickly as possible and be thankful the intelligence sergeant was on the right side. The Case was negotiating its way around a particularly troublesome streak of gristle when Bocker appeared in the door, a scrap of paper in his hand and a troubled look on his face.

"Master Sergeant?" Bocker began, his baritone resonating throughout the small building.

Fetterman, in order to answer, stowed a partially chewed lump of buffalo into one cheek like a chaw of tobacco. "Galvin?"

"We don't have to go hunting that helicopter in the morning. They found it just before dark. But they do want us to send out a patrol to secure it until they can get a salvage bird in.''

"Why us?"

"I think it's because of the crew."

"They weren't with the chopper?"

"Sort of. The Huey was spotted by a FAC who dropped back to take a look. He reported the ship appeared to be in good shape, not crashed at all, but he also noticed there was a body hanging from each rotor blade.''

2

HOTEL THREE, TAN SON NHUT, SAIGON

Even counting their swooping low and zigzagging their way up to Highway One to assist in the hunt for the downed Hornet, the trip had taken less than an hour, yet the difference in surroundings was a radical change. Camp A-555 sat like an angry red zit amid the swamps and scrub of its surroundings, an asterisk on a brown paper bag. Saigon, however, bustled with activity and consumed the landscape with a riot of colors, odors and sounds.

Gerber negotiated his way from the helicopter to a waiting jeep. The Spec 4 at the wheel was sleepy despite, or because of, the sweltering heat and not inclined to conversation during the short drive to the headquarters. A typical REMF, Gerber thought. Probably overfilled with an early dinner, perhaps a couple of cold beers tossed down on top of it and now a safe if boring evening at the wheel. The contrasts between the Special Forces Camp and Saigon extended much farther than mere topography, he reflected.

The building bore the look and character of an abandoned school. Paint peeled, doors sagged on their hinges, and in the hallway footfalls echoed off walls that bore smudgy rectangles where picture frames had once hung. Above all, there was an

ominous quiet that made the walk from the door to the MP-
manned metal gate, and thence to Bates's office, seem longer
than it was and more dreaded. Much of the dread, of course,
was based on prior visits, notably to see and be abused by one
Brigadier General Billy Joe Crinshaw, the beret-baiting des-
pot who had not only tried to get Gerber and his men killed
on several occasions, but who had had the audacity to take full
credit for anything and everything they had accomplished
during his last tour. The Billy Joe Crinshaw who had sent them
into Cambodia had then tried to court-martial several of his
men for being too efficient at their work. The same brigadier
who had taken the morning helicopter to Fifth Special Forces
Headquarters at Nha Trang to announce the charges, then had
himself written up for an Air Medal for the flight!

Gerber's eyes avoided the door that led into Crinshaw's of-
fices, and he quickened his pace. Crinshaw was back in the
World now, making life miserable for a different set of soldiers, but if rumor was correct, he'd gotten some of his own
back recently.

The grapevine had it that Crinshaw had ordered a maneuver during an exercise at Fort Bragg that had ended in disas-
ter for his side. Simulated, of course, but a major wipeout just
the same. As was his habit he'd braced someone he'd felt superior enough to and begun to berate the man for failing to
properly execute orders. The staff sergeant had taken quite a
bit of abuse, then had hauled off and splattered the brigadier's nose!

There were charges, of course, and much screaming and
threatening on Crinshaw's behalf until a superior pointed out
that the enlisted man was a minority, had promised to utilize
every media and political contact available to him at the court-
martial and that this was an election year. No one was certain
what had happened to the staff sergeant, but everyone knew
his name, and he currently drank for free anywhere Special
Forces gathered. Gerber uttered a short laugh at the thought

and promised to buy the guy a whole bottle of his favorite if they ever met.

A streak of light escaped under the door to Bates's outer office, accenting the fact that Gerber hadn't shined his boots before departing. It was a moot point, he reasoned. Bates would be immediately suspect of anyone who managed to stay too strack while out in the field. He took a deep breath, shifted his M-16 into his right hand and opened the door. A weary master sergeant with rheumy basset hound eyes stared up from a crossword puzzle he was working on and took a quick inventory of Gerber as if trying to decide who or what he was.

"Captain Gerber," he finally said, "the colonel's been expecting you."

Gerber nodded, then watched as the master sergeant picked up a field phone that served as an intercom. The NCO uttered Gerber's name into the receiver, nodded at the answer he received, then returned the instrument to its pouch.

"He says go right in, sir. Oh, and he's been up for most of two nights, so don't be surprised if he drifts off on you or gets cranky."

"Thank you, Master Sergeant. I'll keep that in mind," Gerber replied, then pulled the boonie hat from his head and stuffed it into a leg pocket of his jungle fatigues before walking the ten steps to the inner office door and going in.

He was about to salute and report—a nicety forbidden in the field due to the danger of identifying senior officers but a formality some of the old school still appreciated—when Bates put him at ease.

"Mack! Sorry to have to get you out of camp so soon, but I need your assistance on this one. Lean your weapon over there against the wall and take off your webgear. Sit down! You want a drink or a beer before we get started?"

Gerber had known Colonel Alan Bates for years, long enough to know that any conversation that started with the offer of a drink would likely have some unpleasant aspects to it. Of course he also knew enough to take what he could get while he still had the stomach for it, so he nodded.

Bates snatched a field phone out of a pouch nailed to a corner of his desk and barked to the master sergeant seated a mere four feet and one wall away. Gerber wondered why they bothered with the phone, but figured it had something to do with maintaining appearances. The colonel shuffled papers for a moment, giving his guest a chance to stow his gear and settle into a ragged overstuffed chair. The chair looked as if it had escaped the dump more than once, was patched in several areas with green ordnance tape and had a nest of coil springs protruding from one side.

Bates, who'd lost his chance at a star because of the boondoggle in the Hobo Woods several months earlier, was a stocky man with short blond hair. He wore it in a flattop that was beginning to gray. Bates was an old soldier who had learned the new tricks, getting into the Special Forces as soon as he could and staying with it. That could have been another reason he hadn't gotten his star. It still could come, but somehow Gerber didn't think it would.

"Oh, yeah, watch out for that chair, Mack. It bites sometimes. Been meaning to get some new stuff, but it seems I'm always at Nha Trang when the supply boys make deliveries. It's supposed to be a part-time office, of course, but damned if I don't find myself here more often than not. Anyway, we got ourselves a bit of a problem here, Mack. What . . . here we are!" The colonel broke off at the sound of advancing footsteps, which signaled the arrival of their drinks.

A Spec 5, his hair trimmed banker style, the sideburns clipped even with the top of his ears, and the crease in his fatigues sharp enough to be dangerous, entered carrying a mess hall tray with two glasses, a bottle of Beam's and a bowl of ice. Alarms again went off in Gerber's head. First, Bates had begun his spiel with "we," which the captain knew from experience ultimately meant "you," and secondly, the whiskey was Gerber's brand.

"You take yours straight, right?" Bates asked while pouring a healthy three fingers into each glass, then splashing a digit's worth back out when he dropped in a handful of ice. "A damned good thing you do 'cause there ain't a Coke to be found here unless Jerry Maxwell has some hoarded. If he don't, he should be about up to slashing his wrists by now. Cheers!"

Gerber swirled the amber liquid in his glass, then lifted it to his lips. The whiskey's sweet heat flowed down his throat and into his chest, giving a pleasant counterpoint to the slight chill the ice had managed. For some reason, probably the mere fact that it was inaccessible, he thought perhaps a splash of Coke would have gone well with the Beam's. He smiled wryly at the thought of Maxwell going cold turkey, or whatever bona fide Coke-aholics called it. Jerry Maxwell, the resident CIA station manager, had his office in the dank basement beneath them, an office that could usually be found by following the constant flow of ants that homed in on the empty soda cans that littered his desk.

"Now, as I was saying, we have this little problem, see? As I'm sure you're aware, the Marines are up at Khe Sanh keeping company with several thousand NVA. They're surrounded and outnumbered about ten to one."

Gerber took the colonel's pause as a cue that an answer was required. "Yes, sir, been that way for a month or so now. Are things taking an ugly turn?"

Bates's eyes bulged slightly, and he managed to eject a fine spray of Beam's Choice in his haste to respond. "Hell, no! Nothing like that at all. In fact, during the past month and a half our boys zapped over six thousand NVA at a loss of only 190 or so of our own. Pretty damned good kill ratio for troops the papers are assuring the world are scared shitless and not long for this world, huh? They're surrounded, all right, but that doesn't mean what it used to. You see, newspaper and TV folks think in two dimensions 'cause that's all they can produce. They tend to forget the third dimension—airlift."

"We're getting beans, bullets and even toilet paper in and the wounded out routinely. In fact, we're even sending some of them on R and R, for Christ's sake! In a little over a month and several hundred airlifts, we've lost three heavy haulers. But the press manages to set fire to these repeatedly so that they can film their little stand-up reports in front of blazing wreckage. Pisses me off, I'll tell you that!"

Bates didn't have to tell him, but the mention of the press reminded Gerber that he would have to get the colonel focused if he was going to have any shot at rendezvousing with Robin Morrow later. The thought was appealing enough to cloud the dread he'd felt when Bates had begun his ramblings.

"So, all's going well in Khe Sanh and the press is a bunch of irresponsible assholes. Where do, uh, *we* come in?"

"Right, I was getting to that. Well, sir, there's a rumor loose in the five-sided nuthouse that LBJ has decided not to stand for reelection. As you can imagine, there's every sort of power play going on at the upper echelon. Lots of commander-in-chief hopefuls coming up with all sorts of solutions to our problems over here, and they don't cotton much to what's being reported in the papers, particularly what's being said about Khe Sanh.

"The upshot of it all is that the heavy brass is getting worried and wants to do something, anything, to bring the siege to a conclusion. Now, if it was me, I'd say blast the living shit out of the perimeter, pull the boys out, then level the whole area, but that's too practical for politicians. Instead, the guidance we're getting here is to practice a little 'jointness' and make an all-services push up there to bail out the Marines."

"But it doesn't sound like they need bailing out. I mean, Marines seem to thrive on long odds and being surrounded. Something about being able to attack in any direction that way," Gerber said, then drained the rest of his drink and looked at his watch.

"It doesn't matter. A whopping body count is in order, along with chasing the NVA back into their sanctuaries. Good press, happy politicians, happy brass hats, and then we can pull out from Khe Sanh and let them have the damned place."

"You don't think they'd do that, do you? After all the trouble and expense, just walk off and leave it?"

"Sure. It's served its purposes. All we needed it for was to be a thorn in the side to their supply routes, make them go a little deeper into Laos and Cambodia and slow the flow of supplies to the South. Okay, so they moved the Trail a few klicks to the west of the tricountry border. I Corps is happy and ready to pull their boys back where they can do more good. And that's where we come in."

Gerber almost flinched at the "we." Instead, he poured himself another three fingers, braced himself mentally for what was to come and handed the bottle to Bates. "Go on, sir."

"I said they wanted an all-out joint services sort of push. Well, as you know, we've been a little busy around here lately, and there are precious few spare troops lying around to send up there. Even if there were, I don't know where they'd put them. Khe Sanh's not all that big, and the Marines already hold all the high ground. So the best option is the one I mentioned earlier—the third dimension. What's proposed is that we send in more B-52s and let them do some serious urban renewal around Khe Sanh. I'm talking big here, Mack. Remember us talking once about close air support?"

"I think so."

"Remember I said you want to get our own boys for anything real close 'cause they're family and will put a round in your back pocket if you ask for it, right? And the Navy's good for surgical strikes, 'cause they don't have bombs to waste and usually hit pretty close to what they're after, right?"

Gerber nodded at the appropriate places but was beginning to heed the master sergeant's comment about "drifting off." Bates then slapped his desk with such force that the captain spilled most of his drink and started to dive for his weapon.

"Well, by God, this is something different! This will be Air Force BUFFs and it won't be any surgical strike, no sir. This time it's *chemotherapy*!" Bates shouted.

Through the thin wall Gerber heard the master sergeant utter an oath that was brought on by his stabbing a pencil right through a five-letter word meaning *plenty* and into his palm. The colonel was standing now, obviously quite pleased with the whole thing, and the windowpanes still rattled in their frames. Cautiously Gerber tried to prod Bates for specifics.

"Sounds interesting, and long overdue. But what is it you want us to do?"

"Not your boys, Mack. You. I want you to go up to Khe Sanh, get the lay of the land and drop off a few things to help the B-52s find their target."

"Beacons? You want me to go up there and set out beacons? Remember the last time we had anything to do with beacons? Need I remind you that the NVA can triangulate off those things, too?"

"Not beacons, Mack. Reflectors. Radar reflectors. They fold up like umbrellas, are really portable and should be a bitch for the NVA to find since we hold all the high ground. There'll be an RTO and a portable radar site atop Tiger Tooth Mountain that'll check each reflector for you, make sure it stands out on their set. Once the target area is laid out with reflectors the B-52s can come in and paint a whole new landscape up there."

"Sounds like they want to paint by number, if you ask me. I take it this will entail passing through enemy lines and, incidentally, a neutral border or two. How will that sit with your brass hats?" Gerber asked, the shadow of Crinshaw very much over him now.

"That's why *you're* doing it. I need someone who won't get caught."

"Meaning, at no cost. Is that right?"

"You've been there before, Mack. We both have. I don't think I need to tell you, but I will anyway, that what we've discussed here isn't for general consumption. Not even to

Fetterman, and especially not to Miss Morrow! She'll be waiting for you at the Carasel Hotel bar, by the way. She stopped in this morning to see if I had anything for her and I told her I'd called you back here for a day or two. I took the liberty of having a room reserved for you . . . a single.''

"Thanks, I think," Gerber said slowly, aware that a blush was starting to heat his cheeks and wondering if it could fight its way through his tan. "Meanwhile, back to this deal. Am I supposed to hump these umbrellas through enemy lines and up hillsides or what?"

"You'll ride for most of them. Ever hear of Quiet One? Never mind. Suffice to say you'll be working with a special detachment of helicopters. You can rappel, or they'll ferry you in close and come back to pick you up—if you finish in time."

"In time for what?"

"While it's still dark. Didn't I mention that? You'll be working at night. Couldn't have you packing a bunch of tin-foil umbrellas around in the sunlight, could we? Of course not." Bates looked at his watch, squinted, then resumed. "That's the gist of the thing, Mack. Stop by G-3 in the morning for the rest of the details and your maps. Make it mid-morning—no real rush. I don't need you in Da Nang before, oh, let's say tomorrow about 1700. Master Sergeant Rash will handle your transport out of Tan Son Nhut. You just be at Hotel Three after you finish with G-3."

"That's it?" Gerber asked, then tugged a coil spring loose from his thigh so that he could stand.

"Well, there's good luck, of course, but I figure you'll make your own like always. If you need anything, I'll be in constant contact. Now, unless I'm badly mistaken, there's a long-stemmed American beauty over at the Carasel who may or may not have as much patience with you as I've had. So I suggest you save your questions for tomorrow and attend to Morrow tonight!"

Bates found his play on words far more amusing than Gerber thought justified and was still cackling sporadically as the captain gathered his gear and departed. The master sergeant was back at his puzzle, a fresh Band-Aid prominent on his left hand. Gerber nodded a farewell in the man's direction, then thought to comment.

"Guess I'll see you again tomorrow, Sergeant."

"Not really necessary, sir. You're on the manifest for the noon logistics shuttle to Tan Son Nhut already, and there's a hop to Da Nang leaving at 1300."

Gerber nodded, then turned for the door. As he was about to step through it and into the dismal hallway, the master sergeant cleared his throat, as if to say something unpleasant.

"Yes?"

"Uh, just wondering, sir. Do you happen to know a four-letter word for *New England waterfowl*? It ends with an *N*."

Through the door to the inner office came yet another loud bray of laughter as the colonel gave in to his lack of sleep and infusion of liquid spirits.

"*Loon*, Sergeant," Gerber said. "I think the word you're looking for is *loon*."

3

MACV HEADQUARTERS
SAIGON

Jerry Maxwell's attention was divided between the scratchy voices coming out of the small tape recorder, and the alluring triangle of thigh being offered by the young woman seated across from him. At the moment the thigh was winning. Impatiently he forced his attention back to the voices and reached out to shake several of the Coke cans scattered around his desk.

An anxiety bordering on panic came over him as he ascertained for the third time in the past hour that all the cans were empty. He mentally damned the supply types who'd misrouted the weekly supply of Class VI stores, then returned his gaze to the reclining pyramid that was the slit in the Vietnamese woman's skirt.

Brouchard Bien Soo Ta Emilie, known professionally as Kit, passively registered the CIA man's attentions and made no effort to remove his focal point. The cheongsam with its side slits was designed to draw a man's attention, and the fact that it succeeded troubled her not at all. This, she reflected, was no doubt due to her French father's genes, since such exhibitionism ran counter to true Vietnamese mores. The dress, or more correctly what was beneath it, served to keep most men off balance and confused, thereby affording her a slight edge in dealing with them.

At the moment, however, it was she who was confused. Maxwell had sent her an urgent summons and had been even more cryptic than usual in his instructions, allowing only that he wanted her present when he met with a certain man—hence the fiery red cheongsam that she accented with matching stiletto heels and that contrasted with her waist-length raven hair and the almost innocent look of her young, angular face. Passing a violet eye over the huddled mass of olive drab seated next to her, she wondered why she'd bothered.

"Here it comes, sir," the jungle fatigue-attired sergeant promised in a voice that held neither excitement nor anticipation—merely a statement of fact.

The recording continued. "Hornet Ops, Three-Five..."

All three pressed their hands to their ears simultaneously to block out the squeal coming over the tape player as the voice broke off. They looked at one another, feeling silly as one at a time they recognized their parody of the "See No Evil, Hear No Evil" monkeys. Kit grinned at the thought, a show of even white teeth Maxwell found as becoming as it was unusual among members of her race, most of whom chewed betel nuts until their teeth were reddish-brown. Kit's grin soon turned to a grimace as the interference died abruptly and the voices resumed.

"I say again, snakebite. Break-break. Avalon, Hornet Three-Five's inbound to you. Estimate six miles. Do you have smoke?"

Another voice came over the tape, a smooth-toned voice with just a hint of accent that the men thought could have been Midwestern or perhaps Canadian.

"This is Avalon Two. Yes, we have smoke grenades."

"Roger, wait until you hear me and then pop it."

"Okay, will do!"

Then the tape went silent for a moment before resuming the jumbled crackle and banter that was the hallmark of radio traffic in the South. The sergeant rose and shut off the tape machine, then plopped ungracefully back into his chair.

"Well, that's the last one. Judging from the hiss of the carrier wave, I'd have to guess it's a twenty-nine, an URC-10 maybe, but definitely one of our sets," the signal sergeant said.

Maxwell considered this for a moment, along with the implications. "So what are we dealing with here, Johnson? Do we have a Russian in the woodpile or an American gone wrong? I think we can rule out the VC, judging by the diction and pronunciation. Besides, their language school is no better than ours when it comes to stressing the differences between standard conversation and radio telephone lingo. This guy sounds right at home on the air."

"That's what I thought, too. There's a few glitches here and there, but nothing that our own guys don't do routinely enough. What tipped it was the brief passages of gook, pardon me, ma'am, the Vietnamese you heard between English transmissions on the first two tapes. The signal boys up in Khe Sanh noticed there wasn't a key break between them—the same voice spoke both languages."

"Yeah, I heard that, too," Maxwell said, then knitted his brows in thought while absentmindedly shaking the Coke cans nearest him in the vain hope that somehow one had miraculously regenerated its precious liquid. One can did yield a soft rattle, which gave him a glint of hope until he remembered it was just the butt of one of Kit's skinny little cigars. The thought of accidentally taking a swig of that almost gagged him but did serve to remind him why he'd invited her here. He set the can down, returning it to the ranks of the others that formed a barricade against the blizzard of paper that swept across his desk. "Kit, the Vietnamese on the tapes. Can you place the accent for us? I need to narrow it down geographically as much as possible."

Kit's eyes remained glazed in thought, and a dim glow of perspiration was evident on her forehead and upper lip. She hesitated, weighing in her mind a question of loyalties past and present and rationalizing what her answer should be. At last she reached a compromise she could live with, though she wondered who and how many might have to die because of it.

"North, I think. I would say from the area around Vinh. The words spoken you have no doubt already interpreted, yes?" she said, then uncrossed her legs while she rummaged through a small bag in search of another thin black cigar.

The sigh of nylon against nylon whispered a sensuous message to the men as she again crossed shapely legs and the side slits of her cheongsam framed them in crimson. Maxwell was the first to recover and get back to the subject.

"Yes, of course. Just numbers, coordinates perhaps," Maxwell answered, then became aware of the heat in the room. He wrestled his way free from the white tropical-weight jacket that, along with his closemouthed nature, had earned him the nickname "The White Clam."

"Frequencies," Sergeant Johnson said. "The grouping of the numbers would imply frequencies to me. That plus the fact that the numbers just happened to jive with the local comm card. Not too hard to understand where they got them in the first case, but the rest has us puzzled."

"I see," Maxwell said, his eyes now firmly attached to the point where Kit's black hose terminated above her knee to form the bottom leg of the triangle. He became uncomfortably aware of a dull·warmth gathering at his groin and decided to break off his observation of Kit's thigh lest the combination of low blood sugar from lack of Cokes paired with sexual arousal caused him to pitch facedown onto his desk in hypoglycemic shock. "Right! Well, then, Sergeant, what seems to be the upshot of all this? I mean, how's it affecting the war effort?"

"Well, sir, so far it's not doing very much country-wide, but the potential is there. We've had some artillery strikes called in on friendlies by this guy, as you heard on the first couple of tapes, and there's a real possibility that he called down the chopper on the last one, though we don't know that for sure since they haven't recovered the bodies or anything yet. Word has started getting out up north, though, and it's beginning to cause confusion, as you might imagine.''

"Such as?" Maxwell asked as he squinted through the blue haze caused by Kit's cigar.

"Are you sure we should go into this, sir?" Johnson questioned, glancing over toward Kit.

"Go ahead, Sergeant. Miss Brouchard is one of mine. If there's anything I feel she shouldn't know, I'll stop you."

"Well, it's playing hell with support up there. The redlegs don't want to take a chance on throwing rounds in on our boys, so they're having each call for a fire mission authenticated like crazy. Makes it hard on patrols that have been in the bush a few days, since they can't get our daily codes. Ditto in the case of helicopter support. The Dust-off boys have prided themselves on their service, and rightfully so. Up until recently our average casualty in the field was scarfed and on his way to the rear in an average of less than two hours after getting zapped. Now the average is over three, and we're beginning to lose some priority cases due to the time lost while authenticating and reauthenticating. It's really gumming up the works, sir.''

"I see. Well, I guess there's nothing else to be done but to find this guy and put him out of commission, huh? How do we go about it?''

Johnson again looked over to Kit before proceeding. She was seemingly unaware of their conversation, currently entertaining herself by blowing smoke rings toward the basement ceiling.

"We put some units in the air and on the ground to triangulate on him, then, once we have him pinpointed, send in some folks or a gunship to take him out.''

"Sounds simple enough, but what's to keep us from blowing up the wrong guy? You heard it yourself, Johnson. The guy sounds like he's from Ohio, for crying out loud. What's to keep us from misidentifying our target and making things worse than they already are?''

"I've got some thoughts on that, Mr. Maxwell, but I'll need the cooperation of your office and your contacts here with G-1. What I have in mind is an old Indian trick."

Maxwell glanced over the sergeant's head to the mass-produced painting hanging on his wall, which depicted a battle between Indians and the cavalry. The print was entitled *The Hayfield Fight* and was now appropriately framed in an oval of smoke recently released from Kit's lungs. Through the haze Kit looked almost Indian, what with her long, straight hair flowing down the sides of her round face and over the swell of her breasts to terminate in an ebony fringe at her waist.

"Something left over from the Indian Wars, Sergeant Johnson?" he asked.

"Well, not really. More like World War II, remember?"

"Ah, yes, WWII. The big one, I believe they called it. Back when the enemy used real bullets, right?"

"You've been listening to too many big-war bigots, Mr. Maxwell," the sergeant said, then smiled.

"Can't be helped. I have to deal with too many old-timers in this business. It's a toss-up as to who irks me most—the press boys who thrive on belittling our boys' accomplishments or the sanctimonious veterans who view the whole works as some sort of smaller-than-life exercise where no one is really playing for keeps. Anyway, you were saying about World War II?"

"Yes, sir. I'll need a few men I can keep in the field for a while, Sneaky Petes preferably, since they travel light and can be inserted without a lot of coordination beforehand, and some aircrews who are familiar with the area."

"And what area would that be, Johnson?"

"Why, out around the Angel's Wing, of course. That's the last fix we had on this guy, if indeed he was the one who lured that helicopter down. We'll know when the crew is recovered. He has a novel way of treating his victims, Mr. Maxwell."

"I see. Kit? That's out your direction, isn't it?" Maxwell asked.

Kit confirmed the obvious. After all, hadn't Maxwell overseen her interrogation after she'd *chieu hoi*ed in that area? It was an area she'd become intimately familiar with after having escaped her former Vietcong bosses, one of whom she'd personally insured wouldn't be following her, and an area she didn't particularly relish going back into, knowing her fate should she fall back into their hands.

"Kit will work with our ground troops and—"

The nervous jangle of the ancient phone on Maxwell's desk interrupted him. He stared at the heavy Bakelite monster until it repeated its summons, then snatched it from its cradle.

"U.S. Information Service, Maxwell," he said, then merely nodded in response to the caller's words, which buzzed from the receiver. Maxwell's face ashened in response to something said before he rang off with, "Very well. I guess that pretty much confirms it, then. I'll be back in touch shortly and I'll be sending over a Sergeant Johnson who'll need some assistance. See to it he gets whatever he needs, okay? Thanks."

"That was a confirmation of the helicopter lost from Cu Chi. It's our boy, all right. In mythological times the Sirens just lured their victims onto the rocks and let them drown, but this guy...damn! Drop by G-2, Sergeant. There's some folks waiting to help you there, and they'll get whatever you need from Personnel. Meet back with me here at 1700 hours and we'll rough out a plan. Questions?"

"Just one, sir," Johnson said as he got to his feet. "How come *your*, uh, outfit is honchoing this?"

"Well, let's just say there was some concern that maybe another nation was involved that would put it in our house. We don't know for certain that that's not the case, by the way. I hope you're packed and ready to move tonight, because we'll need to head west as soon as possible. Kit? That goes for you, too. After what I've just heard, I think we need to move on this with all haste, Sergeant. If what Kit here says is true, we might net ourselves a big North Vietnamese fish in the process, hmm? Who knows?''

Kit knew. Not only did she know what sort of "fish" it was, she also knew him by name.

4

HIGHWAY ONE NEAR GO
DAU HA VILLAGE

Major Nguyen Bei Lao, unslinging his rifle, sought shelter behind the rim of a small ridge formed by nearly interlocking bomb craters. Through the morning mist, which hung like moistened ghosts, his ears registered the noisy advance of his men. Even over the relatively clear area next to the highway, his men managed to create more noise than a pair of water buffalo mating, and this brought a scowl to his face. Their lack of discipline marked them as what they were—technicians unskilled in the fine art of stealth, which is the hallmark of the successful ground soldier. Lao made a mental note to include a statement to this effect in his report, then concentrated on the more pressing matter of the approaching enemy.

The ground beneath him was soaked, a fact he hardly recognized since he'd spent the past three hours in the dark trooping through the dew-laden brush that bordered this stretch of the highway. It hadn't taken much time for the dank-smelling water to penetrate the last bastion of dryness at his crotch. The feeling was singularly unpleasant, numbing.

As he lifted binoculars to his eyes, he wondered if this was how it would feel to grow old and impotent, both conditions he feared above all else and sought to hold at bay by a strenuous regimen of exercise. A protesting twinge rose from his groin and served to remind him of his last exercise in the latter regard—a young village girl at Go Bac Chien whose father had sent a son to fight for the South. A coarse chuckle tried to escape his throat as he remembered, but he forced it back as the image through his binoculars came into focus.

The line of men ambling along would have seemed ill-formed to the untrained eye, particularly the random distances between the men and the fact that they kept to the muddy shoulders of the road when firm footing was available a scant meter away. Lao grudgingly admired this aspect of the enemy, however, carefully noting how the spacing reduced the potential damage of a grenade or mortar attack. He would make a note in his report that some success could be expected if they mined the shoulders of roads near enemy concentrations.

The thought of mines brought his binoculars forward of the enemy soldiers and off the road to the cover he expected them to take once the ambush was sprung. Slowly he panned the area, noting each significant clump of brush and swale of earth where the enemy would likely seek shelter. The small anti-personnel mines planted at each site were invisible through the glasses.

Satisfied with his preparations, Lao returned to the soldiers and waited until the faces of the lead men came into focus. They were young faces and many of them were black. Lao reflected upon a recent lecture he had given to an assembly of new Vietnamese conscripts at their training camp near Sangker, Cambodia. In this lecture he had sought to teach the new arrivals the ways of the American forces, to emphasize what another Oriental had taught hundreds of years before—know your enemy. The words of Sun Tzu still rang true.

Specifically Lao had wanted these men and women to recognize just *who* the Americans chose to do their fighting, namely blacks, Hispanics and other disenfranchised social groups of their population. He had cited the fact that should an American be intelligent enough, and of sufficient economic standing to do so, he could go to college indefinitely and avoid military service. To emphasize this point he had asked the conscripts to observe how great a percentage of enemy soldiers they had seen fell within these social groups, a fact most had had to agree with. Then he had presented data, citing the small portion of the entire population these ethnic and social groups represented in America when viewed against their percentage on the front lines in this war of American aggression.

The lecture had been well received, and the mix of faces now approaching along the road bore out his premise.

The first enemy soldiers were passing the broken bush that served as the initial point for the ambush. Lao panned to the brush line on either side of the road, trying to locate his snipers. His search proved unsuccessful, a fact that pleased him, so he returned to the soldiers, carefully counting them and trying to make out their unit patches.

There were fourteen, two of whom carried radios similar to the one on the back of the man squatting next to him. The enemy radiotelephone operators had the long whip antennae of their units bent double and secured to their packs to avoid easy detection in combat, and at least one of them, he knew, had an officer walking nearby. The other would likely have the senior NCO next to him, which is why the radiomen and their immediate comrades were the targets of the sharpshooters.

Another of Sun Tzu's observations came to mind: once you've severed the head, the serpent invariably dies! Sun Tzu, however, hadn't foreseen the advent of radios, long-range artillery and air support. If he had, he'd have known just what a many-headed serpent this enemy could be. Now not only must one remove the head, Lao thought, he must also be sure to take out the tongue, as well.

A SNIPER ON THE NORTH side of the road moved the cross hairs of his 3.5 PU scope to the glowing ember of the cigarette that was clenched in his target's teeth. The cigarette reminded him how long it had been since he had indulged in one and how good it would taste. His eye left the scope for an instant and sighted along the barrel of his Russian-built Mosin-Nagant rifle to check his target's position relative to the broken bush.

It was time.

Returning to the scope, he again found the enemy's head and placed the sight post on the tip of the man's nose. He took a deep breath and let part of it out, then held the rest and began to squeeze ever so gently on the trigger until he felt it ease up against the hard point beyond which the rifle would fire. He made a crisp click with his tongue, a signal for the other snipers to take out their targets, waited two seconds for the signal to be repeated down the line, then continued to squeeze.

The bark of the 7.62x55 mm rifle cut the morning air like thunder. The man's head erupted in a mist of bright red before dropping out of the field of sight. Quickly now the gunman moved the sight to his next target, a somewhat older man who had been walking behind the radio operator. The new target had stopped but was still stunned by what had happened and had not yet made a move to seek cover.

Other rifles were singing out their songs of death now as the sniper dropped the sight post to his new target's chest and squeezed again. The rifle bucked and the round caught the enemy full in the chest just as he was turning to run. The impact sent the man backward to land in a disjointed heap in the road, one hand twitching spasmodically as though trying to grasp his weapon, which now lay as harmless as a beheaded snake along the muddy shoulder. The sniper now moved his scope from side to side, seeking other targets and counting the enemy dead and dying. Settling the sight post on the radio pack of his first target, the sniper put three rounds in it.

MAJOR LAO MONITORED the progress of the ambush through his binoculars. Four of the enemy lay still along the road, while

three wounded men clawed their way toward cover with varying degrees of success. The snipers were alternating their fire
as planned, the better to keep the enemy confused and delay
any meaningful return fire.

A yellowish smile parted Lao's lips as an enemy soldier
dived behind a bush, detonating a mine. A portion of the man,
a leg perhaps, went spinning across Lao's field of vision to land
in the road near the others. Then came another explosion,
which was muffled by either the soggy ground or the enemy's
body. The tenor clack of M-16s joined the sounds of fleeing
birds and screaming wounded, signaling the next phase of
Lao's plan.

A click of his fingers summoned the handset of the captured radio, a request the NVA radioman was quick to answer. Lao placed the phonelike handset to his ear and held it
there by leaning his head to one side as he'd learned to do from
observing his fellow students in America. M-16s yipped and
ripped as the enemy fire increased, several on full automatic.
Lao's index finger followed the text he'd written out earlier as
he keyed the microphone and called for artillery support. His
first attempt sounded too flat to his ears, not enough excitement in his voice, so he hurriedly rekeyed and blurted out his
request again, making certain he had left the mike open long
enough to allow the sounds of battle to punctuate his urgency.

The S-3 sergeant on the other end of this conversation traced
coordinates on his map, then stabbed a red pin into an area just
east of the juncture of Highways One and Twenty-two. The
red pin stood out against a yellow background, which caused
the sergeant's eyebrows to knit in consternation. Quickly he
lifted another phone to his ear, this one connected directly with
an artillery battery. After a brief conversation, which was interrupted by Lao's voice coming over the other set's speaker,
the sergeant confirmed coordinates and made an apology that
he couldn't provide heavy fire due to the proximity of the target area to the highway. Lao cursed expertly, then agreed to
adjust fire for whatever they could offer.

The first two rounds were smoke and struck well behind Lao's snipers. The major offered corrections along with the suggestion that additional smoke rounds be fired, since the first were very near his own position. The next rounds hit alongside the road but slightly short of the American positions. Lao estimated there were still four or five enemy returning fire, along with several wounded who were vocally making their plight known. He gave a range correction and watched happily as the first live rounds struck near the enemy positions and sent great gouts of dirt and flame into the gray sky.

"Right on!" Lao shouted into the microphone, the side tone of his voice hurting his ears but reassuring him with its authentic American sound. Then he said, "Fire for effect!"

Volley after volley of shells hit the flats on either side of the road, a display of accuracy that greatly impressed Lao and equally distressed the surviving members of the American patrol. Soon all fire from the Americans had ceased. Lao keyed the mike again.

"Knock it off, knock it off!" he began. "We have broken contact, over."

"Last rounds inbound!" came the reply.

Three more geysers of orange-tinted dirt announced the arrival of the final rounds, and then there was only the squawking of distant birds and the subdued moaning of the wounded. Plumes of white smoke reached into the damp air from bushes set afire by the artillery rounds, and what appeared to be other bushes began closing in on the scene of destruction from both sides. In a calm voice now Lao made his final transmission.

"Last rounds on the ground. All clear here. I have wounded and will need Dust-off. Get him airborne, will you? I'll have a situation report for you in a few mikes, out."

Next Lao nodded to two men behind him who operated the clumsy but efficient Russian-built scanner and homer. These men would monitor radio traffic, identifying frequencies, and then use null homing to plot the positions of the transmitters.

It was crude by modern standards, and required several lines of position to be accurate, but it was effective enough to allow Lao's team to garner the information necessary to carry out strikes such as this one.

The major was satisfied with his results overall and the effect they would undoubtedly have on the enemy. In fact, he calculated that equal success on his return swing north would greatly cripple the Yankee imperialists' operations and earn Lao great accolades from his superiors, perhaps even a promotion. His father, he reflected, would have been proud. This thought brought a bitter memory to mind and an equally vile taste to his mouth. He tossed the handset to the RTO and smirked as the man fielded it poorly and bloodied his nose in the process.

The sight of blood made Lao anxious for the final phase of his plan. If beheading and mutilating the enemy were the foundations of successful tactics, then blunting the enemy's will to fight was the capstone of strategy, or so Sun Tzu had said, though not in so many words.

Checking his wristwatch, Lao estimated he had as few as ten minutes before helicopters began arriving and knew that, without supporting transmissions from the ground, the first in would be deadly gunships.

Ahead he saw his troops bent over enemy bodies, searching for papers, codes, frequency cards and anything else that might be valuable. That the bodies would also yield watches, money, weapons, jewelry and delicious American cigarettes was a bonus that made the miseries of long marches at night and hours of lying in wait worthwhile to his men. The weapons would go to arm more of his countrymen, the money to finance their operations, the jewelry divided according to rank and the cigarettes were Lao's alone. He was particularly fond of the long Pall Malls, a taste he'd developed along with his prowess in English and appreciation of, if not for American values.

Flies were already gathering on the faces and wounds of the dead when he arrived at the scene. The acrid smell of cordite hung in the thick air intermingled with smoke from the burning bushes and the distinctive odor of the corpses, some of which had lost control of their bowels just before death had claimed them. The wounded were gathered in the lee of a large bush; there were only three. Lao spoke slowly and distinctively to his second-in-command, congratulating him on the overall success of the ambush but expressing some disappointment in the small number of prisoners. Then he ordered the wounded men's dog tags removed and brought to him.

Lao studied the thin metal plates briefly, then tossed one set in the general direction of the oldest of the wounded—a black corporal of about twenty years whose glazed eyes echoed the depth of pain raging through his bullet-riddled abdomen.

"You," Lao said to the corporal. "I see you did not ask for this duty. It was unwise for you to allow this to happen to you and doubly unfortunate for your comrades here who came to our country of their own accord. You will see what awaits anyone so foolish as to think your political will can be forced upon our people by military force. Remember this lesson well, Corporal, for I have no doubt you'll be asked to state it repeatedly, and it is my strongest wish that you do so... and often! Now, Comrade Ng, if you will do the honors."

TRUE TO LAO'S PREDICTION, the first helicopters to arrive were gunships. The scene below was all too familiar to the pilots: fresh red gouges in the earth where artillery rounds had landed and the broken bodies of men lying in pools of blackening blood that were alive with flies. When the surrounding area had been suitably probed with rockets and machine gun fire to assure a total lack of enemy resistance, the medical evacuation helicopters landed to take on their grim cargo.

A strange sound greeted the man who stepped gingerly from the helicopter, a low rhythmic moaning that made itself heard even above the whine of turbines and swish of flattened rotor blades. When the source of this sound was located, three of the medics turned aside to empty their stomachs and the fourth stood transfixed.

Two of the three wounded were still alive, though that fact wouldn't provide much in the way of consolation. All three were horribly mutilated and sat staring and sneering at their rescuers through eyes that no longer had lids and, in the case of all except the corporal, with mouths that no longer had lips.

On each forehead two letters were crudely written in blood, the same two letters that began the men's respective serial numbers on their dog tags, on the corporal "U.S." to indicate a draftee, and "R.A." on the others to indicate a volunteer. The other bodies were similarly disfigured so as to defy identification and to deny viewing the remains at their funerals. Still the low-pitched wail continued; it was the corporal singing an old spiritual he'd learned from his mother at age six. But to him the song was newly learned, and his mind would never again allow him to progress beyond that age.

5

CAMP A-555

Fetterman took a long pull from his coffee cup and grimaced as the bitter liquid spread heat and caffeine throughout his already hot body. Then he went back to pushing reconstituted scrambled eggs from one side of his mess kit plate to the other while working up the nerve to take a bite. The powdered eggs were an improvement over the canned variety available in their C-rations, but just barely. At least the powdered eggs were the right color; C-rations tasted about the same but were often an odd green. Finally he gave up on eating and rose to mix himself a glass of Tang in hopes of dimming the effects of the coffee.

Staff Sergeant T.J. Washington, the team medic, beat him to the jar of ersatz orange juice and started to spoon some into a canteen cup, then decided against it. Washington was a young black man who had become the senior medic when Ian McMillan had been killed. He was a big man, with dark skin, dark eyes and dark hair.

"Damn, Master Sergeant! What the hell is this place coming to anyways?" Washington all but shouted, the exasperation in his voice mirrored in his bloodshot eyes.

"Meaning what, Doc?" Fetterman asked, his own nerves stretched thin from the lack of sleep and the general fatigue felt throughout the country due to the sudden surge of operations tempo brought on by the Tet offensive.

"Meaning this chow. Look here. We got powdered eggs, powdered milk, powdered orange juice, powdered coffee and powdered sugar. What I'd like to know is this, is there some new army reg that says troops should be able to *snort* their meals or something?" Washington asked in an uncharacteristic whine.

"I see what you mean. Want some eggs? I have some left that you're welcome to."

"Nah, I say the hell with it. Think I'll have a beer instead."

"Sounds like a plan to me," Fetterman agreed. "Good thing the Army hasn't come up with powdered beer, huh?"

Washington considered this for a moment while he opened two semicold cans with the P-38 can opener on his dog tag chain. He lifted one can and took a long, Adam's apple-bobbing guzzle while offering the other to Fetterman. While the master sergeant sipped at his brew, Washington wiped his mouth with the back of his hand and considered the ramifications of what Fetterman had suggested.

"I don't know. Might not be so bad, now that I think about it. Course if they do beer, you know damned well dehydrated women are just around the corner, and then there'd be no reason at all to let us go on R and R, would there?"

"Save the taxpayer some bucks, I should think. Why don't you drop a suggestion in the box next time you're up at HQ, T.J.?"

The medic released an impressive belch and stared at his beer, his eyes losing what mirth had found its way into them. "Sorry, Master Sergeant. Didn't sleep much last night. I kept seeing those dudes around that helicopter and remembered all the times I took that shuttle to Cu Chi myself to draw medical supplies and such. It's . . . it's a damned shame."

Fetterman, too, had missed some sleep over the incident. It had seemed a fairly straightforward mission at first—a helicopter making a forced landing and setting down right in a VC ambush. God knows it had happened before, and with disastrous results for the crews. But this was different. The crew wasn't just killed; in fact, two men were left alive, and it was they who had caused all the missed sleep.

Fetterman could still see the bodies of the copilot and crew chief suspended upside down from either end of the helicopter's rotor blade, and the way the blade had turned slowly in the light breeze, making the corpses seem as if they were riding some sort of satanic merry-go-round. The impression had been heightened by the two men who sat tethered to a nearby tree, their lidless eyes staring out like gargoyles.

"That it is, T.J., that it is. Warrant Officer Hines was in his last month on this tour, too. Not that it would make any difference *when* it happened, mind you."

"Yeah, that's right enough. Bocker says there's a lot of traffic about it and that the Hornets are working up a bounty for anybody getting the dinks that did it. Probably do some leaflet drops and such, too."

"Don't know that the brass will go in for that bounty business. I mean, what's the odds of getting the guys that did it, anyway? I mean, the exact ones? Pretty damned slim, I'd say. Besides, there's a directive on the street about mutilations that cites some of our boys' ear collections as pretty much the same thing. Sure you don't want these eggs?"

Washington shook his head while draining the rest of his beer, considered having another one, then decided against it.

Fetterman washed his mess kit and returned it to its proper hook before picking up his weapon and stepping out the door and into the sunshine. The newer roofs reflected the harsh light like yellowish chrome, making it painful to look at them for long, while the older tin had rusted sufficiently to give off an orange glow. Fetterman considered going by his hootch and collecting his sunglasses but was attracted by activity in the strikers' area. He arrived as Captain Minh was completing his morning weapons inspection.

"Good morning, Captain Minh," Fetterman said in Vietnamese.

"Good morning, Master Sergeant," the LLDB team leader answered. Not so good. When he used his native language, the British accent disappeared. Minh was one of the few Vietnamese officers whose family hadn't bought him a commission, and who had been trained in Great Britain. After the battle at Plei Soi, Minh had disappeared, but then had wandered into another Special Forces camp. After a couple of months of paperwork, as everyone tried to figure out who he was, he had been sent to the newly constructed Triple Nickel to take command of the Vietnamese forces.

"Problems?"

"I just received word of an incident at Go Bac Chien. The village chief was murdered and several of the women raped. Among the women was the niece of one of my new strikers. Spirits are high for revenge among Nung Tai and Vietnamese alike, so I was on my way to consult your lieutenant about taking out an investigative patrol. Would you walk with me?"

Fetterman read the concern in Minh's voice, along with a loathing that rivaled Washington's. Minh was a professional, a product of the early Village Pacification Program, a well-trained member of the Luc Luong Dac Biet for over three years, and the CIDG for two years before that. For this reason Fetterman found it curious that the Vietnamese officer would display so much emotion over what amounted to a common enemy incursion. Maybe it was the long-term effects of being at Plei Soi when the VC had tried to overrun it, or maybe it was the result of the Tet offensive, he reasoned. But whatever it was, it still wouldn't justify putting Nung Tai strikers in the field with green lowland troops where the natural prejudices of each group might compromise their mission. It was Fetterman's job to say so if need be.

The executive officer was in something of a state himself when they arrived. He'd just received word that Colonel Bates's helicopter was again inbound, and he was torn between wondering whether to feel relieved that Gerber was likely on his way back or worried that perhaps it was the colonel himself. He nodded occasionally as the men put forth their suggestions and would have been surprised if someone had told him he'd agreed to Minh taking a platoon of his troops to Go Bac Chien while the master sergeant and Sergeant Krung took out a night ambush patrol. The situation got even worse when Bocker arrived to announce that the helicopter was only five klicks out.

Minh and Fetterman excused themselves and set out to prepare for their respective afternoon activities, leaving the lieutenant to buff his shoes and sweat. The master sergeant thought about sweating some, too, when he heard the distinctive pop of Huey rotor blades and remembered he still hadn't had his talk with Krung.

Fetterman was in the ammo bunker going over the camp's supply of ammunition for the various weapons, twilight scopes and the batteries, when a familiar voice spoke to him from the doorway.

"While you're in there, see if you have a Fulton unit that's serviceable," the voice said, the words sounding sinister as they echoed around the dormant tools of war.

"What? Maxwell? Is that you?"

"In the flesh. Don't tell me you didn't recognize me, Fetterman?"

The master sergeant blinked back the bright sunlight of the doorway and eventually made out the CIA man's silhouette, though something was different about him, something that took a moment to place.

"What the hell are you wearing?" It was nothing like Maxwell's almost standard uniform of white suit, white shirt and dark narrow tie.

"Jungle fatigues. Not the best fit, I'll grant you, but the best I could do on short notice. You didn't really expect me to wear my normal outfit out here, did you?"

"No, I suppose not," Fetterman admitted. "That white suit would sure stand out here. Speaking of which, what the hell are you doing here, anyway? Must be something really unpleasant for you to give up your home court advantage like this."

"Now, now. I have full authorization from your bosses for this one, and it should be just a walk in the park for your guys. I was serious about that Fulton. Do you have one?"

Fetterman had to stop and think. It wasn't something they commonly used. In fact, it wasn't an idea he personally cottoned to, condoned, or trusted. The Fulton Extraction System consisted of a web harness attached to a wire cable that was in turn connected to a helium balloon. In theory one donned the harness and inflated the balloon, which lifted the cable into the sky. Then a low-flying aircraft with special rigging on its nose snatched the cable and reeled the poor unfortunate into its cargo bay. He'd seen a demonstration of the system at Fort Bragg, using a dummy as a payload. The whole affair had left him with a new outlook on terra firma, namely the more firma a man kept his feet on the ground the less terra he'd feel in his heart!

"We've got one here somewhere, I think, but I doubt it's been inspected for a while, and you know what this climate does to webgear."

"Get it. The passenger I have in mind probably won't weigh that much, so it won't have to be one hundred percent. Nice digs you guys have out here, by the way. At least you don't have to fight pneumonia from excess air-conditioning."

"Thanks. They've renovated some since you were here last. Nothing like having your home burned to the ground to bring out the decorator in you, right? Of course, they've moved the camp, too. A traveling camp. Okay, when do I find out what this visit is all about and who gets to ride the flying jockstrap? And if you say it's me, you're a dead man, Maxwell."

"No, it's no one you know. At least, not yet. You find the Fulton and I'll meet you over at the team shack. By the way, you guys got any Cokes out here?'' Maxwell asked, a spray of anticipatory saliva squirting onto his tongue as he waited for an answer.

"We'll see. If we do, it'll be lukewarm, I imagine. Finally got a decent reefer out here and now the generator's on the fritz. Bogs down at night when we put on the floods, but it usually get things cooled back down by afternoon, so you might be in luck.''

"Great! See you in a few. Oh, by the way, I have a couple of guys I want you to meet, and bring your communications maven with you. What's his name?''

"Bocker. Galvin Bocker. You'll recognize him. He's roughly the size of an M-113 and almost as graceful. And sunburned. Never gets out of the deep, dark recesses of his bunker, or rather hardly ever. When he does, the sun gets to him immediately. Smart hands, though. If he gets there before I do, don't rile him. He doesn't care much for the civilians over here.''

"I'll remember that. See you.''

Fetterman watched Maxwell until he disappeared into the brilliance of the afternoon sunshine. The master sergeant realized that, impossible as it might seem, the CIA man looked even more unkempt in fatigues than in his usual garb. The fatigues were easily three sizes too big and had large sweat-damp areas under the arms and across the back. Standing still, Maxwell looked like an unmade waterbed, but in motion, he looked like a poorly erected pup tent in a monsoon. This last analogy reminded Fetterman where he'd last seen the Fulton outfit and, after moving several bundles of shelter halves, he located it.

The smell of musty canvas reminded him of a small circus he'd seen as a child, a very small circus—even the elephant had looked hungry—and the Fulton flashed his mind back to the Fort Bragg demonstration. The dummy had taken flight so suddenly and violently that its boots had been left behind. Shuddering he left the ammo bunker, holding the bag at arm's length as though the collection of straps and wires were scales and fangs.

"MASTER SERGEANT FETTERMAN, meet Spec 4 Benjamin Willow and, uh, *Sergeant* Dan Stonehand, who I think you may already know."

Fetterman dropped the Fulton unit onto the floor and rubbed his eyes to speed their adjustment to the reduced light inside the team house. The pair of men just introduced were hardly a matched set; in fact, they looked more like a "before and after" commercial for Charles Atlas.

Willow was aptly named. He was a bookish-looking youngster who only came up to Stonehand's shoulder and who seemed to frequent the same tailor as Maxwell. The sergeant's rank insignia on his shoulder bore a telltale dark area beneath the three chevrons where a staff sergeant's rocker had been removed. This item confirmed the man's identity to Fetterman's satisfaction and put a touch of reverence in his voice, and extra strength in his grip, as he greeted the man.

"*The* Dan Stonehand, I presume? I'm sorry my captain's not here to meet you, Sergeant. He's been looking forward to it. Willow, is it? Glad to meet you. No, Jerry, Sergeant Stonehand and I haven't met before, but I know of him through some mutual friends, and all I've heard has been positive, especially his working relationships with superiors."

Stonehand gave a thin smile, and what might have been a blush spread beneath his coppery complexion.

Maxwell looked puzzled, then reasoned that meetings between fellow Special Forces men was probably something of a fraternity thing complete with code words and maybe even a secret handshake. He shrugged it off and downed the remains of a Coke, his second, and moved toward the small refrigerator to help himself to another.

"Okay, Maxwell, let's have it," Fetterman ordered while waiting for the Coke-aholic to feel each can and select the coldest. When viewed from behind, he observed, Maxwell looked quite a bit like a flying squirrel, what with his fatigues hanging in loose folds from his armpits and thighs.

"All right, here's the deal. You ever hear of moon cussers, Master Sergeant?"

"Can't say as I have. Why?"

"Well, way back when ships skirted coastlines they used lighthouses to keep off the reefs and rocks, right? There were some unscrupulous, uh, entrepreneurs, I guess you'd call them, who'd set up a potbellied stove atop hills overlooking rocks and shoals, then open and close its door to simulate a lighthouse. This would lure unwary ships onto the rocks and these men would then 'salvage' their cargoes. They were called moon cussers because they could only do their dirty work on moonless nights."

"You having some trouble with riverine forces?"

"No. What I'm getting at is that we've got an enemy loose around here who knows our comm system and speaks English well enough to call in fire support missions and helicopters. Worse yet, he butchers his dead and mutilates his prisoners, then leaves them for us to find. It's playing hell with morale, and combat support is going to dry up if we don't get him out of action pretty damned quick."

"I know I shouldn't ask, but how did this fall into your lap? Sounds like a purely military thing to me."

"Yeah, well, at first there was some speculation that this guy might be Russian. I mean, his handle on Americanese is straight from back home, and you know the North Vietnamese lingo schools just aren't that good. The guy speaks fluent Vietnamese also, and Kit places his accent as being from the Vinh area."

"Kit?" Fetterman asked, his eyes brightening momentarily.

"Brouchard, you know. She's over with your XO, by the way, getting settled into some quarters. I recommended he put her up in Gerber's hootch, since I didn't know how she'd be accepted among the other Vietnamese. Any thoughts on that?"

"Good idea. No, no problems. I still don't see where you come in on this, though."

"Orders from the top. We want this guy taken alive."

"Whose top, mine or yours?"

"Both. I can get it in writing if you like. Suffice to say the big boys want to keep this out of the press as much as possible. So everything said or done here is compartmentalized out the wahzoo. Makes top secret seem like barbershop gossip. The psy-war boys feel this guy may be an advance test of a whole new scheme of operations. They butcher their victims, then send grossly disfigured survivors home to serve as walking antiwar posters. Not only that, but they select the regular Army guys for the worst treatment while emphasizing to the draftees that they should have beat feet to Canada or turned queer instead of entering the service. If the press picks up on this, it'll play havoc with recruiting and make the draft dodgers seem omniscient."

"Yeah, I can see that," Fetterman agreed. "But why keep him alive? I should think this is one dink even a chaplain wouldn't mind smoking."

"Because we want to talk to him. He speaks English with such fluency that his interrogation would be three times more valuable than any we've had to date. Nothing lost in ambiguous interpretations, nuances, regional idioms . . . hell, he's probably an NVA officer! If he came down here along the Trail, and indications say he did, just think of the light he could shed on enemy operations along the way and in the North."

"Okay, Jerry, I'll grant you that one. I take it that's why you want the Fulton, but why not just walk him out? Presuming we can catch him, that is."

"I doubt he'd surrender without a fight. And we can't take chances on his survival if he's wounded. I emphasize 'wounded,' Master Sergeant."

"The Dust-off boys are pretty reliable, or do you have a particular medical facility in mind?"

"All right, yeah, I do. He's to be flown straight to Tan Son Nhut where there'll be a medical staff waiting, along with a whole platoon of MPs."

"And more spooks than you can shake a rubber hose at, right?" Fetterman asked with a sly smile.

Maxwell looked cornered. He shifted his eyes to his Coke can and spent several seconds inspecting the syrupy stain around its rim.

"There will be representatives of J-2, G-2 and all other appropriate agencies, of course. Did you expect otherwise?"

"No. I can think of at least four reasons why I'd like to see this guy terminated, though, reasons we found on and around a helicopter yesterday. But I can follow orders. Now, how do we go about it and when?"

"I'm afraid there's a lot more than four reasons, Tony. I'll cover everything later on this evening. Meanwhile, Stonehand and Willow will run through their parts of the plan with you—give you all a chance to get acquainted. I'd like Kit to go with Minh's patrol, if you don't mind, just to refresh herself on the lay of the land. And I suggest you cancel that night ambush of yours. You look like you could use some rest, if you don't mind my saying so."

Fetterman minded his saying so, a bit. He also felt Maxwell was overstepping his authority in dictating who went on what patrol and which patrols went out at all. On considering the CIA man's selection of words, however, he realized there were no real commands but rather a host of suggestions. Kit and Minh had worked together before, no problem there, and he really could use the rest. A scrap of intelligence received earlier, however, dictated that the ambush be in place before first light, and he'd rather take it himself than turn it over to Lieutenant Mildebrandt on short notice. He looked around at the expectant faces, noting the two Indians and for the first time seeing the similarity in their features.

"The ambush has to go, Jerry. Some VC supplies are headed this way, and I'd rather face them in their crates than in enemy hands. By the way, you didn't happen to invite these two gents into what you refer to as your 'office,' did you?"

"Of course. Why?"

"Just wondering."

Then Stonehand spoke up for the first time. "If you're worried that Mr. Maxwell's choice of art might have offended us Injuns, don't sweat it. In case you haven't noticed, the cavalry troops are the ones wearing the black hats in that picture, and I guess we've all seen enough westerns to know what that means!"

6

KOMPONG RAU
CAMBODIA

Lao was content to bask in the reflected glow of his own success for the moment, to lie back and accept, humbly, of course, the praise and admiration offered by cadre and conscript alike. Given the limited scale of operations carried on from this minor base, his twin victories over the enemy forces were considered nothing short of inspiring. Much of this, he admitted grudgingly, was a sham—just the local toadies kissing up to a representative of the all-powerful NVA. But he enjoyed it nonetheless, especially the attention lavished upon him by the doe-eyed *co*, some of whom were scarcely sixteen and in the full blush of young womanhood.

The commandant of the camp was most impressed with the bounty Lao's men had laid at his feet upon their arrival. A dozen serviceable M-16s, two M-60 machine guns, a pair of M-79 grenade launchers and a full complement of extra magazines, ammo and webgear were placed in a heap in the red dust before him, enough to arm and equip a complete ambush patrol. As a personal touch, Lao presented the man with a U.S. officer's .45-caliber automatic pistol.

The commandant accepted this offering with the reverence suitable to such a gift and immediately donned the belt and

holster. Pride was evident on the old man's face even after the
heavy weapon had very nearly pulled his loose-fitting pajama
bottoms off him. Wearing a pistol was a visible sign of authority among the Vietcong, and wearing an American pistol
implied successful authority. In return the commandant ordered the slaying of a water buffalo and a feast in honor of his
triumphant guests.

Rice wine flowed and the food was plentiful and hot. Lao
wondered absently about the effects appropriating a water
buffalo would have on the farmer forced to give it up. Granted
the ends justified the means and soldiers had to be fed, but the
loss of such an animal, a young cow, had to fall hard upon its
owner and could hurt cooperation. Cooperation was of the es-
sence here just inside the border of what the Americans called
the Parrot's Beak.

Lao resolved to speak of the matter with the base commandant in the morning and to suggest some sort of repayment,
preferably in kind. This thought reminded him of the hamlet
just to the south—Go Bac Chien. There was livestock there,
and hadn't the village earned the legitimate wrath of the People's Army by sending several of its sons to fight for the op-
position? Lao had already seen to it that they were chastised,
of course, but had he been thorough enough? The loss of their
village chief and a few hours' sport with their maidens was
hardly atonement enough for their crimes. Besides, an army
cannot eat its victories. Another visit to Go Bac Chien would
be both prudent and profitable, since it would allow him to
prove the NVA's honor to the wronged farmer and to under-
score the cost of aiding the enemy to the villagers of Go Bac
Chien.

"Go Bac, Chien?" Lao said aloud, then smiled.

A playful mental sprite sorted through his command of three
languages to humorously interpret the Vietnamese, taking *Go
Bac* phonetically into its English meaning and *Chien* into
French. A throaty chuckle rattled around the small hootch and

caused the sleeping girl next to him to groan and roll onto her side away from him.

"Get back, dog?" He uttered the result of his translations, then laughed again.

The girl completed her rollover, exposing her small rounded buttocks to a patch of moonlight that filtered into the hootch. Lao's eyes seized upon the sight, and he was surprised to find himself already excited from his anticipation and remembrances of Go Bac Chien. Here, he thought, is another opportunity to heighten the reputations of men from the north— at least among southern women.

"I GUESS YOU'RE WONDERING about my little run-in with Crinshaw, huh?" Stonehand asked, guessing correctly.

Fetterman had talked around the subject all evening, choosing to spend extra time on the lay of the land around their AO and on the details of the mission which, he hesitated to admit, would start a scant five hours from now. First he had the ambush to take out, and the trigger time for that was even sooner.

Maxwell's plan seemed almost too easy, two ambush patrols standing by at the helicopter pad while another was airborne or in the field. Other air units would be up and ready to triangulate with their Automatic Direction Finding equipment from Hueys and O-1Es. Should the siren, as Maxwell had dubbed him, decide to take on the airwaves, it should be a simple matter to fix his position and ferry troops into position between him and the Cambodian border to set an ambush. The entire briefing had taken fifteen minutes, another reason to worry.

"Well, yeah. I suppose so. Unless you don't want to talk about it, of course."

"Don't bother me none," Stonehand said, then took a sip of his beer and pulled a face at its warmth. "Interesting, seems the longer the brew stays in the reefer the hotter it gets. Is that possible?"

"Around here it is. Galvin's going to fix it as soon as he can get parts, and Kepler's working on that. You were saying about Crinshaw?"

"Oh, yeah. Well, it was just a simple drop-and-spread type of thing the Eighty-second does all the time. The aggressors were in place and dug in, and we were supposed to go in a couple of hours early and secure our drop zone, right? We're sitting down to chow the night before when our Six gets a summons to come to Crinshaw's HQ on the double. Seems he wants to put us in even earlier so we can scout the aggressor's positions before we head back to the drop zone. It was against the ROE, of course, since the exercise wasn't slated to start until 0600, but Crinshaw insisted we go in at night. You ever make a night drop into the boonies at Bragg, Master Sergeant?"

"Tony. You can call me Tony, Dan. And, yes, I have. Not too bad as long as your jumpmaster knows his shit. The DZ is well marked, and you get good wind drops."

"That's just the point. The DZ wasn't lit, and Crinshaw specifically nixed dropping anything to gauge wind drift that might be sighted from the ground. Not only that, but it was a HALO!"

"HALO?" Fetterman asked, the incredulity sharp in his voice, largely because of his own memory of his last High Altitude/Low Opening jump, which had been into North Vietnam. "He had you do a HALO at night, for an exercise? Jesus!"

"With no windage, no lit DZ. That's right. Our Six protested, of course, but was braced against the wall and read the Articles of the UCMJ, particularly the one about disobeying a direct order. Anyway, we chuted up and were on the flight line at midnight. The aircraft was Air National Guard, and a unit that really wasn't supposed to be involved in the exercise, but the crew was good and had worked a lot of jumps before, so there was no problem there. We went out at twenty thousand in two sticks, planning to move along opposite flanks of the aggressors and meet in the middle before exfiltrating back to the DZ.''

Stonehand paused, considering taking another sip of his beer, then decided against it.

''And? How'd the jump go?''

''Not bad, considering. We got separated, natch, and three guys out of my stick drifted past the DZ and into the boonies. Nothing you wouldn't expect, given the circumstances. We regrouped, minus those three, and moved out. The aggressors didn't even have sentries out! We paper-bombed four gun emplacements and pretty much mapped out the whole works before meeting up with the Six and his element. By 0430 were back at the DZ, relaying all this to Crinshaw's HQ. He wasn't there to take the call, though. He was in bed.''

''Asshole. Sorry, go ahead,'' Fetterman said.

''Yeah, well, I guess we're all entitled to our opinions, and I happen to agree with yours of Billy Joe Crinshaw. Anyway, sunup found us sitting along the edges of the DZ, waiting for the main drop so we could brief them on what was where. We waited until well past H-hour and . . . no drop! To make matters worse, one of the guys who missed the DZ was still unaccounted for and some of our troops were out beating the bushes for him. Then about 0830 we got word that helicopters were on their way to pick us up 'cause the exercise had been bumped to the next day. SFC Clemens—do you know Country Clemens?''

''Yeah, I know Country. He was teaching the SCUBA course when I went through refresher training a few years back.''

''Well, Country found our missing boy. He'd landed in the top of an old snag and cut himself along the inside of one thigh. Lost a lot of blood quickly and passed out. He was barely alive when Clemens found him and didn't look good at all. Our medic patched it the best he could and got an IV started, but it was obvious the boy needed serious help. The choppers came in and scarfed us, then dropped us off right outside the HQ.

Now get this. Crinshaw wouldn't even let the ship with the wounded man go ahead to the hospital, for cryin' out loud! He made us all land at his joint first, looked us over with his little piggy eyes and *then* let them go on to the hospital."

"He called our officers and senior NCOs into his office and started really laying it on us. I mean, he had us braced along the wall and walked around shaking his fist in our faces and screaming. He was pissed because we took out those gun emplacements with paper bombs. Said that wasn't part of his plan. Said he just wanted to know where everyone was, not to cripple them. Our Six pointed out that that part hadn't been specified and that it wasn't fair to blame us for doing what we were trained to do. Crinshaw wanted to know specifically who was responsible for the paper bombs, and the Six wouldn't say. Said he was responsible for anything that went on, since he was in command. Crinshaw wouldn't let up, though, and started to get real abusive toward our captain. So I figured if the Six could take up for his men, then the opposite ought to play, too."

"I can buy that. In fact, I hope to hell my Six makes it back in time to meet you, Dan. He's a straight shooter. Name's Gerber. Mack Gerber."

"I've heard of him. He gets high grades from the troops. As I was saying, I figured I'd take some heat off the captain, and I wanted to get this shit over with so I could get over to the hospital and check on our casualty, right? So I stepped forward and said I was the one who'd directed the emplacements be constructively taken out. Crinshaw was spewing spit and the veins were standing out on his forehead by this time, see? He jumped into my face and said the whole exercise had been canceled because we'd gotten caught going in early and now his ass was in a sling. That much I'd already figured. Then he said, 'You'll learn to play ball with me, or I'll have your Native American ass back in Oklahoma stringing beads with the rest of your whiskey-swilling brethren!' That's when I popped him in the beak."

Fetterman was smiling now, thirsting for particulars. "A good one, I hope."

"Yep, a dandy. He had his face right in my own at the time and was spraying spit as he spoke, which had already pissed me off, so I had to lean back to take a shot at him," Stonehand recalled, something akin to rapture invading his eyes as he did so. "Picked him right up and set him atop his desk. He landed on a fancy pen and pencil holder, by the way. I think it was made from a belt of RPD ammo and had about fifty rounds brazed together in a horseshoe shape. Them shells buried themselves in his big ass, and when our medic cut away his britches, he looked like he'd been attacked by a shark!"

Fetterman howled, a heartfelt laugh that exceeded his meager lung capacity and terminated in a coughing fit. When he regained control of his respiratory system, he wiped the tears from his cheeks and eyes onto his sleeve and asked, "So, how'd you make it out with just one stripe taken? I mean, striking a general officer is pretty stout stuff. Not that you weren't justified, mind you."

"That's just it. Crinshaw got his butt chewed for hazarding our team in an unauthorized night operation and getting one of us butchered in the process. The soldier died, by the way, and if we had gone to a court-martial, I fully intended to make that known to the press, the IG and anyone else I thought might be interested. They already didn't like his getting into a fistfight with an enlisted man. In the end they offered me an Article 15, which would cost me just one stripe, and that for only six months, as long as I didn't take it to a court-martial. Rather than drag our unit through the mud by airing our dirty laundry in the press, I decided to take the deal. In a way I'm sorry about that, 'cause I knew the colonel they'd named to head the court-martial and I knew he'd have seen my side of the ethnic slur bit."

"The colonel was an Indian, too?"

"Hell, no! That wasn't the slur I meant. Shit, I've been called chief and redskin and half-breed for so long, they're almost terms of endearment. What I objected to was Crinshaw accusing me of being from Oklahoma! There's not a Texan alive who would have let that pass without throwing a punch, and I know that Texan colonel would have felt the same way!''

7

HANGAR L-6, DA NANG

It looked to Gerber like a plastic Easter egg on skids, and about as combat ready. The LOH-6, or Loach as its pilots dubbed it, was a militarized version of the Hughes 500 and was rapidly gaining a reputation as the most nimble thing on rotor blades. But this one was different. The tip of each blade had a curved addition he hadn't seen before, and the gearbox/engine compartment seemed to have swollen considerably.

A closer inspection, as the ungainly bird was wheeled out, revealed subtle alterations to both intake and exhaust, along with some lettering on the cowl that disappeared when looked at directly, much as a single star will do. He squinted harder in an attempt to make out the phantom lettering and was again tempted to rip the red goggles from his face.

"If you're trying to read the placard on the engine cowl, don't bother," a man behind him suggested. Then the voice's owner smiled as the Special Forces captain flinched in surprise. "It's painted in International Orange, and it's close enough to red that you won't be able to make it out with your goggles on."

"I see," Gerber began, wondering if the blush he felt work up to his cheeks at having been taken by surprise would be visible through the pilot's red goggles. He hoped it wouldn't.

"Something of a departure from standard aircraft markings, isn't it?"

"Yep. But then this here chopper's not exactly standard, either, and the engineering boys want to make damned sure that, if we auger in, whoever finds us will know to destroy any remains. The placard reads, If Found Disabled or Abandoned, Destroy Completely and Report To: USCINCPAC J-2/3 Via Flash Message. They don't want our technology finding its way into the wrong hands."

"I see. Still seems like you're taking a chance having that Day-Glo crap on the side. Makes a nice aiming point."

"Maybe," the pilot said, then studied his passenger closely.

The passenger returned the favor. The pilot was tall and thin with hair Gerber judged would probably be brown were it not being viewed through red lenses, and which was too long to satisfy any Army regulations currently on the books. He also sported a thick mustache that protruded well past either side of his thin face. Except for the facial hair and the large revolver slung from his web belt, Gerber thought the guy could easily pass for a young Abe Lincoln.

"Speaking of aiming points, just whose side are you on, anyway?" the pilot asked.

Gerber broke off his inspection of the pilot and began one of himself, starting at his feet. Black high-top shoes stuck out below dull black fatigues over which he wore black webgear and harness. To crown his outfit, a dark watch cap was pulled down over his blackened face to where only his eyes would show. The outfit was devoid of any labels or tags, and he carried no identification. Thus, were he to fall into enemy hands, he'd be a nonperson. The old 'plausible denial' routine again, he thought.

"I see what you mean. These are what we call *sterile* fatigues, except for the shoes and watch cap. They were a gift from a friend in the SEALs. I'm Mack Gerber, by the way," he said, then extended a hand in greeting.

"Doug Tibbets. Glad to meet ya. Sorry I couldn't make the briefing with you, but we just did some work on this bird, and I had to do a hover check so we could take her out tonight."

Gerber turned to peer into the hangar and counted at least four similar helicopters inside. As he watched, a soldier on a tow motor pulled the huge doors closed, and one of the several armed sentries assisted in locking it.

"You just have the one?" Gerber asked as they walked around the small helicopter and paused while Tibbets tossed his helmet bag and flak vest into the front seat.

"No, there's three like this one. We keep several regular birds in the same hangar so no one thinks much about it. In fact, if it's busy enough out here on the flight line, we can take her up without anyone noticing anything different."

"I see," Gerber said, but didn't.

"I doubt it, but you will," Tibbets said in a friendly tone, then continued as he went about his preflight inspection. "It's been a long-term project in the Army and among some civilian agencies—I suppose you could guess which ones—and the Quiet One here is the closest we've come yet. The main noise problem with a helicopter is the blades and, as you can see, we've made some radical changes to the tips to keep them from popping."

Gerber nodded while studying the blades.

"The intake has been altered and baffles added, as has the exhaust, and there's some high-tech soundproofing around the gearbox and turbine. Put it all together and we make less noise than an electric shaver, except in high winds, of course."

"Impressive. How come the wind makes a difference?"

"Well, in flight it doesn't really. You see, an aircraft just moves through a body of air, and whether or not the air is moving doesn't really make much difference except in navigation and ground speed. But when we're at a hover everything changes. Now the helicopter is literally fighting the ambient wind to remain over its position, and that can get noisy. Not to worry, though. Nights are usually calm, so we should be quiet enough." Tibbets completed his inspection then continued, "I think it's dark enough now that we can take off our goggles, Mack. No, dammit! As you were! Here comes our friggin' cargo."

The note of panic in Tibbets's voice caused Gerber to instinctively reach for his weapon, then prompted him to blush a second time; he had no weapon. The reason for the pilot's tone became evident immediately. The subdued lights of a jeep drew closer until they pulled alongside the helicopter. Gerber easily recognized the hulking form that slid from behind the wheel, and he started forward to greet the newcomer when Tibbets cut him off.

"No lights on this part of the ramp, sir!" the pilot stated, not trying to hide the contempt in his voice. "We've been wearing these friggin' red goggles for over an hour now to get a jump on our night vision, and one good flash from your headlights there could take us back to Block One."

"I'm . . . I'm truly sorry," Colonel Bates said and, much to Gerber's surprise, meant it. "I just wasn't thinking. I'll watch it in future, okay?"

Gerber couldn't recall ever seeing his colonel so subdued and apologetic, though Tibbets's stern warning did seem reasonable once he thought it through. The way it had been said, however, reminded him that he hadn't asked the pilot's rank. He'd assumed Tibbets was a warrant officer, like most helicopter pilots in-country, but now he wasn't sure.

"Mack, here's your 'brellies.' Take damned good care of them, 'cause these are all the riverine boys could spare. They use them to mark channels down south, I think," Bates explained while pulling a long box from the back of his jeep. "Better practice with one a few times to get the hang of it."

Gerber opened one of the remaining two boxes and extracted one of the reflectors. The thing did look amazingly like an umbrella at first, then more like the retractable reflectors portrait photographers used. The catch on the shaft was similar to an umbrella's, but the canopy would only deploy part of the way, giving the reflector a roughly conical shape. The material was coarse-woven and looked like tinfoil-coated burlap. Satisfied with its operation, he collapsed the unit and placed it back into its box.

"Seems simple enough. Any last-minute details?" Gerber asked, knowing full well an "Oh, by the way" was probably lurking somewhere in Bates's mind.

Again he was surprised.

"Nope. You've got it all. Well, there *is* one thing I'd like for you to do while you're gone," Bates said with a wink, then stepped gingerly back to his jeep.

Gerber was almost relieved. In the years he had known and worked with Alan Bates he'd rarely been sent out on any mission, no matter how unconventional, that didn't get more unconventional at the last minute.

"I thought as much," he said. "Well, what is it this time? You want me to steal General Giap's dentures or something while I'm up there?"

Bates paused and considered this a moment longer than Gerber found comfortable, then hurriedly walked back toward him carrying what appeared to be a club. Gerber wondered if Bates's behavior at MACV headquarters might have been the prelude to his going completely off his rocker, and wondered further if he might have to fend off an attack. The club refined itself into a familiar image, however, and put his nerves back on standby.

"I know this is supposed to be a completely sterile operation, Mack, but I wonder if you'd mind carrying this for me while you're out." Bates handed his captain an AK-47 wrapped in a shelter half.

"Thanks. I'd be happy to. I was beginning to feel a bit naked," he said while turning the weapon over in his hands and inspecting the clip wrapped with it, which was actually two curved clips taped together facing opposite directions.

"I thought as much. Have a good flight, Mack. I'll see you in a couple of days unless there's problems, but keep me posted on how it's going."

"Yes, sir. And thanks again."

Tibbets, who'd been observing their exchange between looks at his watch, now spoke up.

"The gun can stay, but take the canvas with you. I don't want to be cruising along fat, dumb and happy and have a friggin' pup tent sucked up into my rotor blades. Might ruin our whole day!"

The colonel winced again, started to apologize, then merely accepted the shelter half and stalked back to his jeep without a word. Gerber watched as the jeep departed and wondered again what rank this pilot held that allowed him to jump bird colonels as if they were boot privates. Or was he even military?

"Are you in the military, Doug?" Gerber asked the night. Tibbets was already running through his prestart checks. "Are you in the military, Doug?" Gerber repeated after he'd strapped into the left seat.

A smile fought its way out from under the mustache as Tibbets considered the question. "For another ten months I am. Why?"

"I was just wondering. You seemed to put the fear of God into the colonel, so I was wondering what rank you are. Not that it matters . . . sir?"

Tibbets bellowed over the intercom, a rich throaty laugh that easily drowned out the hiss of ignitors and the chirping whirl of rotor blades. "I'm just a wobbly-two, Mack, a chief warrant officer. And I'll forget the 'sir' bullshit, if you will."

"Done. How the hell do you get away with it?"

"Simple. Your colonel was wrong both times. If he'd zapped our eyeballs with his headlights, we'd have had to delay this hop for at least another two hours, and that means scrubbing it until tomorrow. He damned sure didn't want that to happen, let alone have to explain *why* it happened. Secondly, I once saw a helicopter go down on account of a bread sack getting caught on one of its rotor blades. This is a fully articulated rotor system, not like the Huey. We catch something on one blade, it throws the whole works out of balance, sets up bad vibrations and can destroy the ship in a few seconds. Your colonel is a good man, from what I've seen, but at the moment he needs me, and I intend to use that leverage every chance I get. God knows the brass has never thought twice about putting *my* butt in some uncomfortable places, and *yours*, too, I'd wager.''

"True enough. But what's to keep them from just getting another pilot and farming you out to ferry honey pots?''

"That's simple, too. You'll see." Tibbets then reached into a pouch beside his seat and pulled out what looked like a pair of jeweler's loupes joined together in a frame. He attached this contraption to his helmet.

"X-ray vision, Doug?" Gerber asked.

"Close. Night-vision goggles. You've got a set and a battery pack beside your seat, but I'll warn you, you might be better off not watching. It's kinda scary at first.''

"We'll see.''

And see he did, Gerber had to admit. Through the night vision goggles the main compound of Da Nang fell away beneath them, but not nearly so far away as he would have liked. Even given the surprisingly clear view through the goggles, an effect that was increased due to the time spent in the red lenses, Tibbets seemed to be keeping dangerously close to the ground. The sound level in his helmet was a weak testimony to all the silence engineering, though most of it was the normal gravel and wheeze of in-country radio static. A huge palm ahead of them caught Gerber's attention.

"How 'bout that tree, Doug?" he said with as much calm as he could muster while mentally counting the coconuts clinging to the tree and trying not to visualize them scattering like billiard balls when they hit them.

"It'll pass to your side. Nervous?"

Gerber waited until the tree had slid past before answering. "A bit. I'm having some trouble adjusting to these things. We use Starlight Scopes for night ambushes and forward patrols, but it just isn't the same somehow."

"I know what you mean. We've lost a few guys because of it, too. Your depth perception is not so hot through these so you have to learn to adjust. Takes quite a few flights to get good at it. They claim this is spin-off technology from NASA, but it's got CIA written all over it if you ask me. Anyway, the next model is supposed to have Forward-Looking Infrared, FLIR for short, built in. That should really be interesting, huh?"

The captain flinched as another tree passed his door. What, Gerber wondered, could possibly be more interesting than sliding along in the treetops at over a hundred miles per hour—in the dark? The world outside was an eerie mixture of sharp and muted images, which seemed to fade into nothingness well short of the horizon, a fact which made the pilot seem all the more foolhardy and convinced Gerber that some amount of showing off was probably in progress.

"Well, if you're trying to impress me, it's working. Shouldn't we be up a little higher? I mean, for safety's sake."

"Absolutely. I'm not crazy about this worm-burner route myself, Mack, but we have to stay down here until we clear the Da Nang approach corridor. We're not running any lights, to keep them from screwing up our vision, and we're not squawking our transponder, to keep Da Nang Approach Control from screwing with us for leaving without a flight plan. As of now, we just don't exist. Once we're clear of their turf, we'll pop up a couple of hundred feet and both breathe a little easier," Tibbets said calmly, then turned slightly to avoid yet another giant palm tree.

"How long do you make it to our AO?" Gerber asked, more to gauge the possibility of taking a nap than due to any anxiety.

"About an hour and a half if we were to go straight there. That's not practical, though, since we don't carry enough fuel for the return trip. So we're stopping at Camp Carroll for fuel first. We can shuttle out of there until we're finished."

"Think we can get it all done tonight? That's a shitload of umbrellas for one night."

"Of course not. What I mean is—and I take it from your answer that this is a point your colonel didn't bother to mention—we're to stay as guests of the U.S. Marines at Camp Carroll until we've finished the operation. We can only operate at night, you know, and if I were to bring this thing into Da Nang in broad daylight, my CO would have my butt for lunch!" Tibbets's voice crackled over the intercom.

It was news to Gerber, all right, and it gave him something else to worry about. He didn't mind staying with the Marines—that part was easy enough and they had enough in common to get along. But the fact that Robin Morrow would be arriving in Da Nang at noon the next day did bother him. Again he cursed the weak moment that had made him agree to that arrangement. But then he remembered the magic moments that had followed, and he was soon transported back to the previous evening at the Carasel.

In his sleep he could almost smell her perfume and feel the faint breeze from the slow-turning fan above their bed. A few times during his hour nap Gerber groaned a word or two, but these were lost in the soundproofing and the night. Tibbets didn't notice since he was busy scanning the ghostly ground outside, though he did occasionally check his gauges to make sure the fan currently over their heads *wasn't* a slow-turning one.

8

OVER THE PLAIN OF REEDS

Morning mists still swirled over the loose-knit system of canals below as the sun crawled into the sky, giving a deceptively peaceful appearance to the countryside. Even after the sun had burned off the mists, the ground passing beneath the helicopter looked relatively peaceful to Ben Willow. Sure, there were occasional pockmarks where bombs had landed, each flooded and complete with a small black duck waddling about—a sight so standard in this part of the country that one was tempted to think a duck came with each bomb—but these were nothing compared to where Willow had been stationed until the day before.

A radiotelephone operator with B Company, 1/9th Cavalry, Willow had become accustomed to screaming his transmissions over the constant concussion of artillery from both sides during the past month. So accustomed, in fact, that his first transmission from the helicopter had made every crew member jump. He smiled at the recollection and continued to comb the canals and swamps beneath him with eyes that seemed older than his face.

From their low altitude he could make out the faces of the village folk they passed over, and another contrast came to mind. These people were going about their business largely as they had always done, while to the north the Bru tribesmen of Lang Vei were forced to cower behind whatever cover they could find. Many Bru had already starved or died at the hands of General Giap's army, which had descended from the surrounding hills like a horde of rabid dogs. Many in Willow's unit had also died, a final contrast that overshadowed his initial feeling that, after all the grief it had caused him in life, he'd finally gotten a good deal out of being Cherokee.

"Time to check in," the copilot said as he pivoted in his seat to look Willow in the eye.

Ben nodded agreement, an exaggerated gesture that caused his ill-fitting flight helmet to rock back and forth on his head comically. He consulted the piece of paper in his pocket on which he'd written the call sign he was to use, committed it to memory, then prefaced it with the Cherokee word for *winter*. The resulting transmission sounded like most others, the first of the message seemingly garbled and the remainder clear. To the other units, each of which had a Cherokee soldier monitoring the set, it identified the originator beyond question.

Galvin Bocker grease-penciled a check mark next to Crusader Twenty-eight on his network roster while Stonehand confirmed receipt of Willow's transmission. Another unit working farther south along the Mekong checked in next with a negative report and a request to RTB for fuel and crew switch. This aircraft's call sign brought a smile to Stonehand's leathery face.

"Roger, Tansi. Request for return to base approved. Say ETA back on station."

"I make it one plus zero-zero, over" came the crackling reply.

"Roger, Tansi, back in one hour. Fontana out." Then to Bocker he said, "Show Hornet Two-Four en route back to Cu Chi for fresh gas and ass. Should be back up in an hour or so."

Bocker nodded silently while diligently printing the codes onto his plastic-laminated roster; Captain Gerber's critique of his handwriting had made him conscious of this and, even if the captain was no longer his commanding officer, he didn't want to catch any more guff from him about it. When it came to putting the operational call sign down, however, he had to ask. "How do you spell—what was it?—Tawn-zee?"

"Tansi. About like it sounds. We had it lucky, you see. When Sequoya came up with our alphabet, he didn't have to contend with all the crap English has gone through with your multiple spellings for the same sound. *Tansi* is spelled T-A-N-S-I. Means *big river*, by the way. Pretty apropos for the area adjacent to the Mekong, don't you think?"

Bocker was too busy block-lettering the word to think much about anything, so Stonehand continued. "You've heard a derivative of it, you know. Tennessee! Tennessee is just a bastardized . . . excuse me . . . a white man-ized version of *Tansi*. Most of your states have either Indian names or New something-or-other, which means they're named after another city somewhere else. An amazing lack of imagination on the parts of the founding fathers, huh?"

"Do you always talk this much?" Bocker asked. "I mean, you always hear about you guys being the 'strong silent types,' and every Indian I've ever seen in a movie had less than nothing to say, and when they did it was brief. Hell, Tonto just used subject and verb!"

"Tonto, my ass! If the truth be known, Tonto would as likely be a member of one of the lost tribes of Israel than anything native to America, Galvin. It's just another of the stereotypes we've had to live with ever since you folks stopped shooting us in our sleep," Stonehand said, then emphasized his good nature by laughing and punching Bocker in the shoulder playfully.

The move took Bocker by surprise, but he managed to put on a decent smile after he picked himself off the bunker floor and slid back into his folding chair.

"I haven't been in the Army long enough to be blamed for that, Dan."

"Agreed, and I've never personally been shot at in my sleep until I came over here, now that I think about it. I suppose I do talk too much. Maybe it's all those generations of grunting and trying to get along in a foreign tongue in your own country that's finally coming out. Who knows? The next generation of my people may all be auctioneers!"

"Or lawyers," Galvin added thoughtfully.

"God knows we could use some. Think of all the land we pissed away for nothing! Well, having been to New York City a couple of times I think maybe we got our money's worth on that one. Maybe one day the Cherokee and that lost tribe of Israel will be doing business cheek by jowl. Goldstein, Silverheels and Cohen. Black Bird, Yellow Bird and Rosenberg. What do you think?"

"I wonder if the role of Tonto is currently open. I might apply for it myself."

ON THE PLAIN OF REEDS, Master Sergeant Fetterman lifted his hand and silently made a fist. Fifty meters to his south, Sergeant Krung returned the signal, then extended his forefinger and thumb into a parody of a pistol, which he "fired" at Fetterman. The master sergeant gave a thumbs-up to indicate agreement that the ambush would start when he fired his weapon. Fetterman's eyes traced each detail between Krung's position and his own, noting the crescent placement of his soldiers and their fields of fire as well as the fallback positions they'd take should they have to break contact. And he paid particular attention to the claymores, which sat like flattened, off-color bullfrogs along the banks of the canal.

A fat water snake slithered noisily beneath one of the mines while he watched, nearly tipping it onto its back. The claymore rocked back onto its wire legs and remained pointed out on the canal as the snake flopped ungracefully into the water and swam along the bank to pass directly below Fetterman's position.

The master sergeant wondered if it was an omen and, if so, whether it was good or bad—and for whom? There were warriors who put great store in the actions of animals and elements prior to battle, he remembered. Napoléon had studied his stars, Patton had walked the prospective battlefield and revisited it through one of his prior lives, and Indians, like the one currently lying nearby ready to feed bullets into an M-60, went so far as to consult nature on the eve of battle.

Fetterman shook himself out of his reverie while remaining as motionless as a stone. If any of the Nung Tai strikers had seen the snake and were animists, they could make their own determination as to what it meant. For himself, there was merely the matter of waiting until the three approaching sampans were opposite the claymores, and then he'd control the fates of as many on board as possible with three quick twists of his wrist.

To his dismay, the snake slid up the bank nearby and slid out of sight. Only a widening V remained on the water to mark the reptile's passing, another omen perhaps and he couldn't help wondering whether it stood for *victory* or *venom*. A shiver of repulsion worked its way up his spine as he heard the snake rustle the fallen bamboo leaves on the bank not three feet from where he lay. The shiver ran the length of his nervous system before translating itself into a spasmodic hand movement.

The first claymore erupted, sending its wire legs backward into the woods and its load of metal pellets across the narrow expanse of water and into the middle sampan. The force of the projectiles carried the canvas side of the sampan's cabin away and hung it like a dirty shroud in the bamboo on the opposite bank. The VC manning the pole at the bow stood straight up and tracked the flight of his cabin before reacting. The second mine intercepted him as he dashed for his weapon, the explosion detonating his cargo and ultimately clearing the decks of the two remaining boats.

Fetterman buried his face in the mud and tried to get even lower for cover. A wave of heat flashed over him from the explosion, followed by bits and pieces of weapon and warrior alike careering through the trees.

Shrapnel and sampan continued to rain as Krung lobbed an M-79 grenade into the lead boat, which was now dead in the water. Fetterman cranked the last claymore into life and was rewarded with sunshine as it took the canopy out of the trees overhead. He cursed loudly, sending the snake fleeing into the water and a well-placed string of rounds following it.

The dotted line of projectiles neatly joined the point of the snake's V, and there was one less serpent in the world. The staccato voice of a Russian-made RPD joined the symphony of racket briefly before yielding to the tenor spat of a half-dozen M-16s. Krung administered a coup de grace to the last sampan with his blooper, caught the last two enemy soldiers as they attempted to scramble from their sinking vessel, and then there was silence.

"Casualties?" Fetterman asked with obvious distaste for the word.

"None!" came the answer after a moment.

"Good. Now, I need two men in the water to fetch bodies and check the cargo on that last sampan before it sinks completely. Washington and Kai? Cover for them. Watch the other bank. Smith, take the rest and fall back to cover our rear. And see if you can get us a ride home."

Smith, the RTO, ambled past the master sergeant's position on his way to the rear with the radio. He paused for a word. "You guys make these things look easy, Master Sergeant," he said.

Fetterman looked into the young man's eyes and wondered if he'd ever been that young himself. If so, it had been more years ago than he cared to count, and the past two had to count extra, he decided.

"As your field SOP says, 'A well-thought-out and executed ambush is the most effective and manpower-conservative operation in warfare and should be used whenever practical.' Not bad, considering we didn't have time for a rehearsal.''

"Not bad? Hell, I think it was *perfect*! I mean, no casualties on our side, and we got all three boats and their crews. How could it have gone better?'' Smith asked, still wide-eyed with adrenaline.

"Well, for one thing, we took some return fire. If this had been a textbook operation, that wouldn't have happened,'' Fetterman stated calmly, then started to add that he hadn't anticipated the exploding sampan knocking the last claymore flat on its back where it would shred the canopy when fired, but decided that discretion was as much a part of modesty as valor.

"Yeah, well, if you say so. Anyhow, if you get tired of your job up at MACV SOG, I'll bet our Six would be tickled pink to have you back here on a permanent basis.''

"Thanks, but no thanks. Captain Gerber and I have spent our time at A-555. We don't mind coming back for a few days so your bosses can take some briefings, but I don't think either of us will be back permanently. At least not in this lifetime,'' Fetterman almost whispered, though why he bothered, given all the racket the men in the water were making, he couldn't say.

"I think I know what you mean. I wouldn't swap a cushy job at HQ for some hole in the bush, either,'' Smith said, then turned to follow the others to the rear.

When he heard excited voices in the river, Fetterman turned abruptly and flipped off the safety of his weapon. He stood and relaxed when he saw the cause of the excitement: the water snake was drifting slowly downstream past the men in the water. Amazingly both men had managed to climb up and were now standing on the point of the last sampan's bow, an area scarcely the size of a football. While he watched, the bow sank under the men's weight, causing a renewed bout of expletives and what was possibly the second and third greatest walks on water ever witnessed by mankind.

To their credit, the men managed to hold on to their weapons and items taken from the dead during their flight. Now they were smiling at their own timidity, and Fetterman felt like joining them at the water's edge. Perhaps he'd wade into the relative cool of the rust-hued canal and rinse some of the crusted salt from his sweat-soaked fatigues. Then he noticed that one of the men was Krung, and saw him pocket trophies from his two kills.

9

CAMP CARROLL, I CORPS

Morning was entirely the wrong time to try to sleep. Even for someone who'd spent the night dangling from a helicopter, it was almost impossible. Mack Gerber rolled onto one side and inverted the rolled-up poncho that served as his pillow, pressing its cool underside to his cheek. The poncho didn't have a cooler side at this time of day, and it stuck to his face. Irritated now, he completed his turn onto his back and lay staring up at the low ceiling. The ceiling was made of corrugated tin and logs over which the prescribed depth of sandbags was stacked against mortar attack. A 4x4 rumbled past, releasing a fine mist of sand from every tin seam, mute testimony to the fact that the Marines hadn't yet received the new rubberized sandbags. But then Marines were usually the last to get anything new.

The sand found his skin and stuck to it in gritty little patches that defied all attempts at removal. It had also found his hair and worked its way right down into his scalp. Reluctantly he pushed himself to a sitting position and swung his legs out onto the dirt floor. The maneuver sent blood rushing down his body in a precipitate flight that left him light-headed and tempted to flop back down in his sandpile for another shot at sleep.

"Not yet," he said to no one in particular. "Not until I get some water on this head, such as it is."

Tibbets, sound asleep across the aisle, broke the rhythm of his snoring long enough to smack his lips twice, utter a guttural groan and break wind with authority. The pilot unconsciously deemed this greeting enough for his senior officer, but added another pair of smacks and a throaty noise, which sounded to Gerber like a cat trying to pass a hair ball, before regaining total oblivion. Gerber was jealous. From force of habit he pulled the camouflaged band from across the face of his wristwatch to compute how much sleep he'd missed. Surprisingly he learned he'd done better than he'd thought.

"Eleven hundred? Eleven o'clock?" he said softly through dry lips. "Sure enough! Eleven hundred, eleven o'clock. And for you Marines out there, Mickey's big hand is on twelve and... Better watch that shit around here!"

Tibbets farted concurrence.

The knowledge that he'd had almost five straight hours of sleep perked Gerber up considerably, though his eyes were still stinging as though he hadn't had a wink. Coffee would help, after a quick soak of the head, he thought, so he quietly got dressed.

First he had to shake out his fatigue pants before donning them, then closely inspect each boot and sock. As unimpressed as he might have been with his boudoir, he knew from experience that several ill-tempered jungle creatures rated crumpled clothes and soggy boots as four-star accommodations. The ritual completed, he grabbed the AK-47 from under his bunk and started to depart. Then he looked at himself and decided that someone, *anyone*, dressed in black would probably be well advised not to amble out into the presence of U.S. Marines carrying an AK-47. He returned the weapon and tried to stalk silently past the sleeping pilot's bunk, which at the moment smelled like the leftovers from an Eskimo picnic. Gerber stood in the doorway for a moment to adjust this eyes to the light, then stepped out into the sun and let the screen door slam behind him.

"Screen door? With a spring yet?" he exclaimed. "Maybe the leathernecks aren't the last to get things after all!"

A crisp report filtered through the screen as Tibbets agreed in his own fashion.

After the brief homecoming visit to Camp A-555, Camp Carroll seemed huge. The camp flowed in traditional order with A Company nestled up against B Company and so on, with a well-ordered arrangement of bunkers and fighting holes interspersed throughout. Given enough time, Gerber thought, the USMC would eventually bring order to this sprawl of real estate and have the world-famous "birdie on the ball" emblazoned on every rock and tree. The Army, he reflected, merely *occupies* ground; Marines bend it to their bidding and impress their will upon the very landscape, then they *hold* it.

The unmistakable smell of coffee interrupted his search for whatever passed for a shower here and sent him at a quick march through the compound. The smell was emanating from a large consolidated mess hall and, more specifically, from a huge pot over which was hunkered an even larger mess sergeant. There was something sinister about the way the man stirred the pot, something vaguely reminiscent of cartoon cannibals about to serve up a missionary, and the fact that the mess sergeant happened to be a mahogany-skinned giant with a partially shaved head enhanced this image. Gerber stopped short as the giant's eyes locked onto his own.

"Smells good, now, don't it?" the mess sergeant said, stating the obvious with equally obvious pride.

"Better than that, Sergeant! Could you see your way clear to part with a cup of it?"

"Now I just might, providin' I can figure out who it is I'm a-givin' it to."

Gerber did a slow scan of his black fatigues, taking in the fresh sweat stains that were quickly gaining on the previous high-water marks of the night before. "Gerber. Mack Gerber, U.S. Army Special Forces,'' he said, then fought an urge to draw himself up to attention and salute the coffee. It smelled that good.

''Well, now, Mack Gerber, I reckoned that might be what you was. An' I guess I can let you have a dab of this here brew, but only as much as you can drink! Set yourself down. I'll draw you up a cup to get you started, and if you want more, I might just join you for one.''

The mess sergeant rattled around under a solid-looking bench affair until he located a canteen cup. He gave the ladle a couple of good strokes to get the grounds swirling, Gerber assumed, then dipped a steaming cupful out of the caldron with a practiced motion and set it in front of his visitor.

''Special Forces, huh? Know what? Firstest time ever I heard of you folks I thought for sure they'd said Special Services! Now ain't that a hoot? Yessir, I surely did think that's what they said—Special Services. Figured you guys went around a-playin' Ping-Pong and countin' bats and gloves. Reckon you don't do no whole lot of Ping-Pong playin', now, do you, Mack Gerber?'' The big man smiled with a perfect ice tray of teeth, which was accented in eyes entirely too peaceful to belong beneath such an awesome brow.

''No, I guess we don't at that, Sergeant...Woodward, is it?'' he said, straining to read the faded black stencil on the cook's T-shirt.

''Woodard. No *W*, sir. It *is* sir, right?''

''Well, yes, I suppose it is. But anyone who can make coffee this damned good can just call me Mack.''

''That's what a lot of 'em says, about my coffee I mean. 'Cept some of 'em say, 'Anybody what can make coffee like this here can call me Sweet Thang, if they's a mind to!' Heh, heh!'' Woodard exclaimed, then let go a booming laugh that rattled around in his broad chest until it brought tears and a dishcloth to his eyes. ''Sweet Thang, yes, sir, that's what they say. Well, I got me some things to do, so you just enjoy your coffee and I'll get to it, sir. Hope you don't mind the *sir*, sir, but it don't hardly seem right to go callin' you anythin' else. I mean, you're an officer and all, and Special Forces to boot. Special! I like that, I really do. Don't care much for your duds, though. Reckon you're up to some of your 'special' stuff hereabouts, huh?''

Gerber breathed a deep breath of the soothing vapors coming out of his cup and marveled at how the extreme heat of the cup felt divine even in the sweltering heat of the day. "I guess you could say that, Sarge," he replied, then again wondered at the unbridled goodwill resident in the big man's eyes.

"Thought so. Wouldn't have you decked out like that to pass out catchers' mitts at the diamond or umbrellas at the golf course, no, sir. Special. I do like that. Yes, I do," Woodard said as he walked off to resume his clanging of pans and opening of cans, which was soon augmented by a gospel bass voice any choir would cherish—albeit lent to a bawdy Marine Corps song.

Umbrellas! If the mess sergeant only knew, Gerber thought. Over five hours of staring through night vision goggles at the hills and valleys that were the Annamese Cordillera, occasionally having to retire from the area while hordes of NVA and supplies traveled down the infamous Trail, choosing the right tree or ridgeline in each area and then rappeling down from the silent helicopter and planting the umbrella. It was different every time but, like sex, the first time stood out in his mind as a never-to-be-forgotten event.

"You sure you wouldn't rather we land and you climb the damned thing?" Tibbets had asked.

"You ever try to climb a tree while carrying a thirty-pound umbrella? You're sure you can hold this thing steady for a while?"

"We'll see" was the pilot's answer.

"Not exactly encouraging, Doug."

"You'd rather I lied?"

Gerber thought about that for a second while he rechecked his harness, ropes and clips, then he shrugged. The gesture was lost in the darkness. "Okay, here goes. If I get into trouble, I'll key the Fox Mike twice to signal I'm cutting loose and three times for you to lift me out. Got it?"

"Gotcha," Tibbets said, then shifted his concentration from the distant horizon to Gerber's face. "Well, is that it?"

"Is that what?" he asked as the pilot again swung his alien-looking visage forward to stare into the distance through his awkward goggles.

"Don't you guys say something before you go out? Geronimo or something like that?"

"Hell, no. Oh, I might say something like, 'Don't try this at home, kids. These men are trained professionals,' but never anything so corny as Geronimo!"

"Get your ass out of here, Mack," Tibbets said.

"Geronimo," said Gerber.

The downblast of the rotor wash was heavier than he'd anticipated and caused him to hunch his shoulders and clutch the thin frame of the door until he'd adjusted enough to reach back in for the first reflector. Then things really got interesting. Habit prompted a person to hold a furled umbrella with its point down, and if there's one thing that had been beaten into him over the years it was the fact that people lived, and died, by habits. Before this experience, in fact, he'd have been tempted to say this particular pearl of wisdom had been about driven into the ground. Then *he* nearly was.

The rotor wash filled the reflector immediately and pulled him from the skid as it opened. Looking back on it, it was remarkable that he'd managed to hang on to the wildly gyrating chute, but the combination of Tibbets's earlier warnings about things getting pulled up into rotor blades, coupled with the adrenaline rush inherent in stepping out onto more than a hundred feet of dark air, enabled him to do it. He kicked out as he went and fell for a full two-count before braking, then hung there spinning around until he stabilized.

The reflector actually proved valuable in stabilizing on this first drop, though he'd made damned sure the thing was fastened shut securely thereafter. The difficult part, of course, was getting back up, and it got progressively harder each time. All in all he was satisfied. They'd planted eight of the things in a rough horseshoe starting at the shoulder of Tiger Tooth Mountain and arcing northwest then south to an area abeam Hill 881N. With another good night's work, he reasoned, they'd be finished and he could get back to Da Nang and . . . ?

"Thought I'd find you here. Why didn't you wake me up?" Tibbets asked.

Gerber blinked back his memories and thoughts of the future and focused on the tall warrant officer. "Morning. You were having so much fun in your sleep I thought it would be a shame to disturb you. Anybody tell you that lethal chemical weapons are forbidden in this theater of operations?"

"Huh?"

"Never mind. Get Sergeant Woodard to lend you a cup. This is the best damned coffee this side of the World."

"Have to get it to go, Mack. I just stopped by the operations shack and there was a message for us from your boys."

"Oh, shit," Gerber said weakly, knowing that if things had gone as well as he'd thought, there would be no word at all. The reward for a job well done is no more punishment. "Let's hear it."

"You know those eight brellies we put out last night?"

Gerber rubbed a sore muscle in his shoulder, which remembered quite well. "Distinctly. Don't tell me. They want to move the damned things, right?"

"Nope," the pilot said, then took an appreciative slurp from the steaming cup Woodard had offered him. "You're right! This *is* the best damned coffee this side of the World! Hell, compared to the swill we normally get this stuff ought to have a name all its own. You know that?"

"I think they call it Sweet Thang. You were saying?"

"My eyes feel like I've been carrying them around in a tobacco sack for two weeks, Mack. Those goggles kill me after a couple of hours. How's yours?"

"Dandy. Now, what is it with the damned reflectors? They don't want them moved?"

"That's just it. About half of them already have."

Gerber's mouth dropped open at this, then snapped back with a moist plop, much like the sound of a perch taking a bug off the surface. Then the muscles at the corners of his jaw started to work in and out, prompting another fishy reference Tibbets would have made had not the captain's voice held so much venom when he spoke. "Charlie found them?" he said through clenched teeth.

"Wrong again. Monkeys."

"*Monkeys?*" Gerber screamed, interrupting Woodard's rendition of a current ballad, which started with "Give me an *F!*" and then progressed into an antiwar anthem all soldiers came to enjoy. "Fucking *monkeys?*"

"Yep," Tibbets confirmed. "Radar boys noticed the first one go down right at first light, then another, so they called in some photo birds. It took them quite a few passes to figure it out, but there it was, a big monkey sitting in the top of a tree looking like Mary Poppins. They got a charge out of it, bet your bun on that."

"They'll do well not to mention it around me, Doug. Let's go see what the wizards from Saigon have in mind."

On their way out Gerber stopped to thank Woodard for his hospitality and to mention that they'd be there a while longer in hopes he'd offer an invitation back. He did. Then, as they were leaving, the mess sergeant couldn't help but ask. "I know this is probably something *special* and maybe I got no business knowin' and all, but did I hear you say something about monkeys?"

"That's right, Sarge," Tibbets answered. Then he lowered his voice and added, "The captain here says he hates fuckin' monkeys!"

"So I heard," Woodard said softly. Then he almost whispered, "Maybe he ought to give it up!"

10

GO BAC CHIEN, RVN

The distinct odor of woodsmoke cut through the thick air as they neared the village, a smell that indicated the morning meal was being prepared as usual. Lao held up an open hand, then listened with lips pursed in disgust as his minions continued another three paces through the brush before coming to a halt. Highly unprofessional, he thought, but he expected no less from this crude collection of technicians and farmers. There was a saying in the real army, he reflected, that one does not get what he *ex*pects, but rather what he *in*spects! He would make it so. But first there was the matter of the village. A gash of a smile parted his grim features as he recalled the predawn brief.

"Go Bac Chien is little more than an insect bite on our country's backside!" he'd said sternly, then paused for the tittering that followed to calm down before reversing himself. "But even the smallest bite can become filled with fever devils, can it not? And cannot the fever carry off even the strongest warrior?"

The men of the village followed their pistol-packing commandant's lead and agreed loudly while brandishing the new weapons and marveling at their slight weight.

"So, are my brothers of Kompong Rau content to sit here with their backsides exposed while the faithless wasps of Go Bac Chien send their sons to sting you?"

The men were equally vehement in their disagreement, some pausing in middenial to hawk and spit for punctuation.

"As you know, my cadre and I have already taken a step toward chastising these...wanderers. To return them to correct thinking, we found it necessary to remove the man who led them, feeling that by removing the misguided head they would find the correct path on their own. But does cutting away the head stop a wasp from stinging?"

His listeners' voices rose as one to deny this and, when their orator didn't proceed, they said it even louder and repeatedly. Lao was content to listen for a time to their coarse voices rising to a crescendo, to savor the fruits of his eloquence. But then the yells began to wane and a few of the men started relating accounts of being stung by beheaded wasps.

"So what are we to do, men of Kompong Rau? Men of the *new* Vietnam? Men of the *future*? What are we to do about Go Bac Chien?" he implored.

"Kill the body, too!" cried one.

"Cut off the *new* head!" reasoned another.

"Burn Go Bac Chien!" suggested a third in a singsong voice that soon began a chant.

Lao admired his handiwork, the hatred reflected in ugly shadows on each face around the fire. Now he could do anything he wished. This was even more of an accomplishment, considering Go Bac Chien was so near and that some of these men might even have relatives living there. The Cause made the difference—a party line, of course, but apparently a true one if the fire-lit wraiths who now screamed for blood were any measure. The people of Go Bac Chien would likely be massacred, if he let these men have their way. But now he would mold them even more to his purpose by showing that their brethren of the North had compassion as well as contempt.

"No!" he shouted, then held both hands aloft for silence. The chanters gave in reluctantly. "No, we will not burn this village, nor will we slay them all. For if we do, Go Bac Chien will cease to exist, and lessons taught to the dead are never repeated! And a lesson is what Go Bac Chien *will* have! We will show them what they can expect as traitors while at the same time leaving them as a village, an entity. Let them know that all must suffer for the crimes of the few, then leave them to correct those few by their own means. Agreed?"

There had been no argument and even more enthusiasm than before. Perhaps this was because some did, in fact, have relatives there, Lao thought, breaking out of his reverie, and he vowed to remember this ploy when dealing with isolated cells in the future. Now the village lay before him and at his mercy.

A light drizzle rattled against the stiff leaves of the upper canopy in a dull roar that sounded like frying bacon, which contrasted with the much quieter sound of it falling in the open at the edge of the jungle. He stepped forward two measured paces until the rain could fall directly upon him and stood there soaking in its coolness. A water buffalo calf bellowed a plaintive cry to its mother somewhere on the other side of this small collection of thatched huts, followed by the musical laughter of children. An older child scolded the youngsters and summoned them inside. Lao recognized the voice as female, then smiled again.

"No one is to be killed unless they offer resistance or try to run away, understood? And do not cripple too many by beating. Cripples are of no use to the future of Vietnam. We will deal with the new chief, of course, but beyond all else, I want at least one healthy buffalo left alive to replace the one we ate in celebration last night, and perhaps another to celebrate our victory tonight!"

The men agreed enthusiastically, if inordinately loudly considering the situation. Then Lao stepped aside and summoned the irregular group's leader forward. "This victory will be yours, my friend. My gift for the hospitality you've shown myself and my men.''

The older man stumbled forward, beaming a smile stained with betel nut as he unholstered his new pistol. He waved the heavy automatic high over his head, then stepped forward in a spirited trot that denied his years. Lao waited until the main body of soldiers were past, then halted three of his own men. These he placed as a rear guard to cover their escape route, should they need it, and to monitor both the UHF and HF bands for radio traffic. Once satisfied with their positions, he strode grandly into the village with the long strides he'd admired in the American troops he'd served as a houseboy in his youth. The Enemy. The same men who'd seen to his education in their country; the same men who'd been responsible for the dishonor and ultimate death of his father. The thought put hate back into his heart, along with a thirst for revenge and a physical need for violence.

"No more men go! No more men go!" a terrified man was screaming when Lao rounded the corner of the first hootch.

Two of the Kompong Rau soldiers had the man's arms pulled behind his back, while a third clutched a handful of hair to hold his head back at an uncomfortable angle. There was already blood on his face, some from his nose and some from a split lip.

The commandant brandished his new pistol in the man's face and again asked how many men the village had sent to serve as puppet soldiers in the South Vietnamese army. The rest of his men were busy gathering the remaining farmers from their hootches and herding them into the center of the village, where a large kettle hung from its chains over a smoky fire. The hot coals sputtered like distant machine gun fire in the light drizzle.

Lao strode over to where the men struggled and eyed the captive passively. He recognized the man as the son of the dead chief, a fact born out by the man's own eyes as his head was released roughly.

"You remember me, yes?" Lao asked slowly, then smiled at the new terror that contorted the man's slender face. "Yes, you remember me. You'd kill me if you could, wouldn't you?"

The new chief couldn't decide how to answer this, nor even if he was expected to do so. To reward him for his silence the commandant brought the heavy barrel of his .45 down across the bridge of the man's nose, shattering it. Blood flew across the faces of the two soldiers holding the man, causing them to release him. He sagged to the mud like a dropped puppet. Lao began to chuckle, a deep angry sound that would scarcely be taken for laughter, a rasping noise that was more like the panting of a dangerous animal. He drew one foot from the mud, scowled at the sucking noise it made, then sought to aim a kick at the bleeding man's head.

The battered face rose as if to greet the blow, causing Lao to hesitate in delivering it. The eyes above the bloody pulp that had been a nose fairly burned with hatred now and fixed resolutely to Lao's, then he hurled himself from the mud and into Lao's chest. The move caught them all off guard, and Lao, poised on one foot with the other suspended behind him, was off balance, as well. The wind rushed from Lao's lungs in a shrill screech as his attacker buried his head in Lao's ribs and both men crashed to the ground. Before Lao could regain his breath he felt sharp teeth bite into the flesh of his chest and sought air enough to scream. A fist found Lao's diaphragm before a breath, however, and now he found himself on the verge of panic. He wanted to shout for assistance, to bellow outrage, but instead he concentrated his strength on pushing the biting, scratching demon from atop him.

Lao succeeded in rolling over but hadn't anticipated his tormentor trying the same maneuver. The men completed two full rolls in the soft mud, which covered them both so much that they were indistinguishable to the spectators. A soldier who had been inspecting the cooking pot hefted his rifle by the barrel to strike the uppermost man in the mud but was stayed by an order from his commandant. Lao had his wind now, along with a handful of fingernails sunk into his abdomen. The nails kept working in his flesh, probing, seeking a hold farther down. New panic seized Lao as the nails rent his flesh. Adrenaline surged through his body, trebling his strength. Though blinded by mud, he reached out with both hands for the fingers approaching his manhood. The hand there was like wrought iron, resolutely clamped to his flesh and unyielding to his efforts.

His fear a palpable thing now, Lao left the hand and pulled the man's head up against his own with such ferocity that he split his own lip on the man's jaw. He felt the hand slip another inch down his belly and under the waist of his loose trousers and could almost feel the clawlike nails digging into his groin and sinking, twisting. With a spasmodic jerk he seized his adversary's jaw, then twisted it until a muddy ear brushed against his cheek. The fingers were past his navel now, scratching, clawing. He uttered a small whimper, like that of a cornered animal, then snapped his head around to bring the muddy ear into his mouth. Biting down, he tasted coppery blood mixed with the dung flavor of mud.

The hand halted its advance, and the man's scream sent a ringing through Lao's head as both men stiffened. The major rolled the new chief off him, spat the ear in the man's general direction, the quickly wiped the mud from his eyes with the heels of his hands. The new chief was writhing in the mud now, one hand clutching the scalloped ear, which spouted blood between his fingers, and the other pulling him forward blindly. Lao stood, spat again, then stepped forward softly. The man pulled himself forward another few inches, then released the ear to wipe at his eyes. Lao stood over him, his chest and stomach streaming blood from a tangle of deep gashes. He held an American Ka-bar knife in his hand. The man saw this and sought to pull himself farther away, but his next grasp found the coals of the cooking fire. A quizzical look came over his muddy face as the nerves in his hand sought to fight through a wave of desperation and into the man's brain, a look that turned into a screaming rictus as Lao's foot came crashing down on his arm, forcing the hand deeper into the hot coals beneath the cooking pot.

"AS I SAID EARLIER, the village must accept responsibility for the actions of all its members and the innocent must therefore suffer along with the guilty. In this way you will learn to police yourselves," Lao said to the gathering.

Although washed clean of the mud, he still felt the heat of embarrassment on his cheeks each time he looked at his adversary. His discomfort wasn't mitigated by the man's size, half again his own, nor by the simple fact that he had bested him—had, in fact, reveled in his vanquishment by standing on the young chief's arm and repeatedly striking him unconscious with the butt of his knife until the offending hand was burned to a blackened, withered claw. Lao could still taste the blood and mud in his mouth along with the bitter bile of panic that was slowly being replaced by the sweet taste of revenge. He warily eyed the man who was now suspended off the ground nearby, his arms and feet bound firmly to four bent-over stalks of bamboo, which were each a hand width in diameter and longing to stand erect. Nearby a girl of twelve years hung similarly suspended, spread-eagled two feet off the ground by arm and ankle. But she was horizontal and facing the earth.

"It is right that the innocent in this case is the guilty man's daughter, and equally right that I, the vindicator, shall choose which one shall pay first.

Lao waited until the soldiers had shepherded the others back to the village. While he waited he ran cautious fingers over the tender welts on his abdomen, following them slowly and painfully down to their terminus below his navel. The feeling was a dichotomy of pain and relief that the grooves stopped where they did. He closed his eyes and started to offer thanks to any gods that might be responsible, then took himself in hand. A soft whimper came from the girl, along with a creak from the bamboo as she sought to readjust her weight. Lao felt himself grow rigid in his grasp at the sound.

"Ah," he said to the chief, "you'll regret not having longer arms to complete the job, my friend. Or should I entertain your daughter by having you offer her to me? Perhaps even beg me to take her as I wish and order her to do my bidding. I can do that, you know. The Death of a Thousand Cuts, the Chinese call it, and I'll guarantee you'll forget all about that hot hand of yours before I'm finished. Do you believe me?"

The girl let go a sob, which hung in the wet air a mere second before being swallowed up by the damp earth beneath her. Lao felt himself pulse. He quickly stepped out of his shoes, the single-thong sandals fashioned from old car tires that he hated but wore to appear more in keeping with the locals. Next he slipped off his soggy trousers and shirt to stand on the hillside in the cooling rain. The village chief was barely conscious and hung from his tethers, a slackened and diminished lump. Lao's gaze flowed down his own ruined body to the excited part he'd saved, then shifted to the girl. She still wore her loose-fitting black pants, but the rain had soaked them to near transparency. They clung to her, revealing the rounded buttocks of nascent womanhood, a fact confirmed by the small, firm breasts that hung beneath her, a fat drop of rain clinging precariously to each pointed nipple.

"Listen well, Father. That which you most dreaded in life will ring in your ears as you die!"

The man didn't offer any reply, nor did he understand Lao's sinister intentions, for he was unconscious and Lao was speaking in English. The man's seeming indifference lessened Lao's excitement, so he reached into his gear and drew out the Ka-bar. With a smooth stroke he brought the point of the knife down the length of the sole of the man's foot, in response to which the man fairly danced among the bamboo and brought a heavy shower of raindrops from its leaves. Lao roared with laughter, then went silent as the girl uttered a desperate cry.

"That's right, you're next. In fact, you're *now!*" he said, then jabbed the knife into the instep of the wailing man and walked again with measured strides over to the girl.

With a single swipe of his hand he ripped off her pants, then turned to hurl them at her father. A fresh howl of anguish issued from the chief, which echoed down the hill and was heard by all in the village. The soldiers took this as a signal and began their own version of retribution, selecting women at random and beating the men senseless.

The girl swam in the air before him, her feet and hands making small circles that set her breasts to jiggling and her buttocks grinding seductively. Lao stepped forward in the Y formed by her spread legs and grabbed her roughly by each thigh to steady her gyrations. His pulse was pounding through his temples now, drowning out the rain, the girl's protestations, even her father's pleas and threats. There was no gentleness in his hands as he pressed each thigh out to its side to reveal the object of his passion, no care as he poised himself to plunge into her, and no accounting for the sudden increase in noise he felt as well as heard as gunfire erupted in the village below.

11

CAMP A-555

"How many does that make now, Krung?" Fetterman asked.

The Nung Tai looked up from his trophy board to consider this intrusion, then went back to his work. "Your counting is still hard for me. I have places for two more," he said in even tones, though he thought the question was somewhat rude. A man's vengeance is his own affair.

"Two more and you will have avenged the loss of your lieutenant, right?" the master sergeant said, working his way up to the real point. "Then you will no longer take these trophies from your kills?"

Krung again looked up, sensing there was more of an order than a question here. He said nothing, so Fetterman repeated it in Nung dialect, and as a statement this time. "Two more and your lieutenant will be revenged. Then you will stop taking trophies, Krung."

Krung's eyes locked onto his. There was a mixture of contempt and confusion in them. "But I am still to kill the enemy, yes?"

"Of course," Fetterman said, wanting to add that he was merely relating an order from higher up, but knowing that wasn't the way professional soldiers worked—each order must be given as though he had decided upon it himself. It was a hard thing to do many times, an unpopular thing, especially so when the orders were inconsistent. He knew only too well what the VC had done to Krung's family and their village, and to his lieutenant, and knew that had their places been reversed he, too, would want revenge in kind. The inconsistency, though, was that Krung was being told it was acceptable to kill the enemy, to maim, disfigure, dismember, even to decapitate if necessary, to kill them, yet not acceptable to touch their bodies once they were dead.

"And I can kill them any way I must. Is that right, Sergeant Tony?" Krung asked, then stood to his full height, which placed him almost at eye level with his American counterpart.

"Yes. But you must agree not to . . . uh . . . *bother* them after they're dead."

"If you say it must be this way."

"All right. Now, have your men fall in for weapon inspection in half an hour. Is Captain Minh ready to debrief his patrol?"

"Dais Uy is speaking with the pale man now. He should finish soon."

FETTERMAN FOUND MINH and Maxwell in the team house along with Kit. Minh was standing in front of the acetate-covered map, tracing his patrol's route with one long finger while the CIA man lounged in a folding chair nursing a lukewarm Coke and a red-hot sunburn. Kit sat apart from the two men on another chair, an M-16 held loosely across her lap with its barrel pointed at two huddled masses squatting in the corner. One of the prisoners wore the fatigues of the North Vietnamese army, and one leg of these was split to above his knee. A field dressing covered the man's calf and someone's go-to-hell rag served as his blindfold. The other wore the black pajamas of the Vietcong.

"Gentlemen, and ladies," Fetterman said as he came through the door, "can I sit in on this?"

Jerry Maxwell pivoted in his seat and squinted at the sunlight pouring through the door. His face, usually the ruddy color of a tourist in the tropics, was now bright pink on the cheeks and forehead and a violent reddish-purple on his nose.

"By all means. In fact, I think you'll find what these two gents back here have to say quite enlightening. Grab a chair."

Fetterman nodded to Minh, then turned toward the far corner to pull a chair from one of the small tables. Kit nodded to an empty chair beside her, a gesture he found extremely feminine despite her fatigues and weapon. Her onyx-colored hair was soft and long, falling well below her trim waist when fully released, but today it was stuffed beneath a boonie hat with only random strands hanging out. She looked tired, and he reasoned she welcomed him to help watch the prisoners.

Minh continued to trace the advance of his patrol across the northern limit of the Plain of Reeds, which paralleled the Cambodian border, to where they had crossed Highway 258 and approached Go Bac Chien from the north. In keeping with policy, he'd sent scouts ahead and kept his troops dispersed in the jungle alongside the road as they had advanced, all the while maintaining radio silence. Half a klick from Go Bac Chien the first of his scouts had returned to report soldiers in the village. Another scout had rejoined them soon thereafter with the NVA prisoner in tow. The counterattack on Go Bac Chien had met little resistance, since the enemy soldiers were mostly irregulars and had been caught completely unaware as they had looted the village. An odd point, which Minh found particularly interesting, was the fact that the enemy soldiers all carried M-16 rifles, most of which had jammed early in the fight.

"The VC prisoner we found hiding under a hootch," Minh said in a clipped voice, while pointing at the man. "And he is wearing a U.S.-issue holster. An empty .45 pistol was found in the village also. In interrogation he admitted being the commandant of a small cell working out of Kompong Rau, but he denies he led either assault on Go Bac Chien. He will not name their leader, but I'm certain he is an NVA officer.''

''Perhaps they'll remember more once we get them to Saigon for further interrogation. What size unit was in the village?'' Maxwell asked while warding off a hungry fly that was trying to get at the oily salve on his face. ·

''Is his name important?'' Fetterman wondered aloud.

''Might be if he's one of Giap's lieutenants. Could mean an advance force in the area sizing up Tay Ninh or Cu Chi for an operation similar to what's going on up at Khe Sanh. Go ahead, Minh.''

''There were maybe twenty-five soldiers inside the village and evidence of others in the nearby jungle. We found two villagers on a small hill to the west of the village who had been tortured. One was the village's new chief and the other his daughter.''

''Could they tell you anything?'' Maxwell asked. ''How many others, what weapons they carried, how they were dressed, anything?''

''They could not tell me *anything*, Mr. Maxwell, because they were dead! The chief had been tied to four large bamboo, which were bent to near breaking. When we made our assault on the village, I assume his torturers cut the muscles between neck and shoulder and across his stomach because he was pulled into three pieces when our scout found him. As for the girl . . .'' Minh stopped and looked at Kit whose face bore sol-·emn testimony to the severity of mutilation the girl had exhibited when she'd found her. ''The girl's throat was cut and a knife left in her . . . uh . . . anyway, both were recent kills and still bleeding, so I assume they died about the same time we entered the village.''

''I see.'' Maxwell said softly. ''Anything else?''

''We killed thirteen and captured three. Two of the captured chaps were wounded and one of these died before we left the village. Twenty weapons were recovered, mostly American, but a few AKs. There were no automatic weapons and no mortars.''

Maxwell wondered, but didn't voice, if the other prisoner had died in interrogation. It was common enough in the field where the need for hard information was paramount and the most time-effective interrogation methods were often brutal.

"The NVA prisoner was carrying this when captured," Minh continued, pointing at a nondescript piece of equipment on the floor. "You may inspect it if you wish, old boy. We've checked if for booby traps."

Maxwell rose from his seat and drained the sugary remains of his Coke, then eyed the gear warily. It was slightly larger than a normal radio and had an unusual antenna that could be turned by means of a small folding crank near the top of the main box. Another oddity, he noticed, was the absence of a power supply, an anomaly that was solved when he found the input receptacle along the bottom of the unit where a battery cable would connect.

The device was devoid of labels and placards that would identify its country of origin, but the general design was definitely Soviet Bloc engineering. Confirmation of this came when he snapped one earpiece off the headset and found a number with Cyrillic lettering on the plastic diaphragm and a word in Czech on the molding. Maxwell smiled, thinking how proud his old language instructor at the FLI would be that, after all his years in the Orient, he could still recognize Warsaw Pact languages.

"It's a direction-finder, what is called a null homer," said Maxwell. "Pretty crude compared to some of our stuff, well, compared to some of the Russian stuff, too, to be honest. We'll let Bocker take a look at it to make sure, but I think he'll agree it's set up for FM. That's a directional antenna, see? Once a signal is received, the operator turns the antenna with this crank until the signal fades out—nulls—then he turns it the other way until it does it again. The problem with this sort of unit is it only gives one line of position, and that can be misread backward since there's a null both ways. That means there has to be at least one other unit in operation to fix a position on the transmitter, or several if you want to be accurate."

Fetterman sat up suddenly and started to ask a question.

"That's right, Tony. This just might be our boy! Now, Captain Minh, if you'll assist me, I'd like to try my hand at getting a tad more information from our NVA friend. I think we need to put a name to our mysterious siren who seems to have such a diversity of interests in this area."

Minh and Maxwell walked to the back of the team house and lifted the NVA soldier roughly to his feet. The man stumbled on his wounded leg, falling heavily on Maxwell, who accidentally kicked out while trying to recover his balance. The man sent up a shrill howl of pain as the foot dislodged his bandage, and the air filled with the keen odor of ammonia as he lost control of his bladder.

Fetterman studied the wound from his seat and easily put a name to the weapon that had caused it—M-16. The weapon's light round traveled at such velocity that it invariably tumbled once it entered its target, causing much more damage than one would normally attribute to such a small projectile. In this case the bullet had entered the man's calf from behind, roamed around in the muscle for a bit, then shattered the tibia on its way out, an extremely painful wound and one that would be only too easy to exploit for information.

"You are hurting?" Minh asked when the man had stopped screaming. "We have morphine, old boy. You would like some morphine to take away the pain and we would like the name of the leader and how many radio units like this one he has. It is a fair trade, yes?"

The man bit down on his lower lip and remained silent. A dark stain crept outward from his crotch, and a thin rivulet of urine crawled from beneath his ripped pant leg and over the gaping mouth of the wound. Another cry escaped the man's throat as the ammonia mingled with the severed nerves of his shin.

Kit's eyes were glassy as she watched this, as though she were looking right through the man and into the future, but it was the past she was seeing. The immediate past of that morning, to be exact; the ambiguous feelings she'd felt when the NVA soldier now weeping openly before her had stumbled out of the jungle ahead of the other scout, only to fall at the captain's feet when prodded forward. The wounded man's eyes had rolled in his head as he had tried to voice his hurt through the tape binding his mouth, and she had felt a twinge of guilt upon recognizing the tabs on the man's collar. They said this man belonged to an NVA unit near her old home in the North, and the softness of his hands marked him as a technician rather than a farmer-soldier, a man of education. The fact that she had until recently been on the same side as this man hadn't entered her mind at all, just that here lay a fellow countryman in pain. Then she had remembered the girl.

She had been moving around the village along with four other soldiers when they had walked upon the scene, and the sight was still too vivid in her mind's eye. The man's torso hung in two pieces from atop still-swaying bamboo stalks while his lower body remained suspended between two others. His intestines reached upward in an unbroken string as though attempting to communicate between the sections. She realized the man's death was fresh when she saw there were no flies on the carnage. A nearby sound raised the hair on the back of her neck and caused her to dive for cover in the bamboo thicket, and that was when she came face-to-face with the girl.

The child's eyes were open and her mouth formed a scream that had never left her slashed throat. The head was almost severed from the body so that it sat on the remains of her neck at an impossible angle to stare Kit straight in the face. Beneath the body a bright pool of blood was gathering, and viscera hung in limp ribbons, but it was the knife that caused Kit to release the scream the dead girl had been denied. And it was the knife that caused her to shed any remaining loyalty to her former masters and to stand now and speak.

"Stop," she said softly. "I know the name you want."

12

CAMP CARROLL, I CORPS

"Because we *need* one, that's why," Bates said patiently, as though he were explaining something obvious to a very small boy.

"Who's *we*? It would appear there's more than enough out there to satisfy everyone at Khe Sanh with a few left over, so who's the *we* that thinks they'd like an NVA soldier all their own, hmm?" Gerber asked in much the same tone.

"G-2, G-3, G-5, all the usual pogues. Who did you think?"

"Oh, I don't know. Says here in the *Stars and Stripes* that McCarthy did so well in New Hampshire a couple of days ago that the administration is worried about its chances next fall. I figure maybe they want a bon-i-fied gook to replace Mc-Namara so they can really flush this thing down the shitter and be done with it!" Gerber spat out with vehemence.

"Watch your mouth, *Captain*," Bates said through clenched teeth, though if asked he'd have to agree with Gerber's view on the SECDEF. "Anyway, it's just an ancillary tasking. If you happen to see one you can grab, do it. Preferably one who's heading north."

"North?"

"North. G-2 thinks General Giap is pulling out his 325C Headquarters and maybe as many as five regular regiments.

This word is allegedly based on secondhand information from a source in Giap's own headquarters as passed to a courier who walked right up to the wire and *chieu-hoi*ed three days ago. Seems there was another defector a month ago who tried to warn them about Giap's intentions, and he was largely ignored. So the brass wants to verify this one and thinks HUMINT is the best way to do it. If you can get them some human intelligence, do it, but the reflectors are your main job. We're redefining the Khe Sanh TAOR as a final step in bringing this operation to a close and opening the next one."

Gerber looked over at Tibbets, who was busy scratching himself and seemed oblivious to what the colonel was saying.

"Which operation is this, anyway? Crockett? Ardmore? Scotland? Seems like every time I hear anything about this place it's called something different," Gerber complained, then realized his voice was very near a whine. The past two months had worn down his patience. Hopefully it wouldn't affect his judgment, he thought, then sought to shift his attitude a bit. "Sorry. I slept well this morning, and I'm having a hard time dealing with it."

"Understood. It's still Operation Scotland. At least it was when I left this morning. And Niagara, Operation Niagara. That's what the Air Force part of it is called, unless that's changed, too. Next comes Operation Pegasus, then Scotland Two, or is it Scotland *Too*? It'll all make sense when it's over, Mack."

Gerber couldn't help but smile at this. It was a standard response these days and came as close to catch-22 as anything in twenty years, but it was SOP.

"Right. Now talk to us about monkeys."

"Would you have believed two days ago we'd be having this conversation? Monkeys, Christ!" Bates said while shaking his head in resignation. "Okay. Here's what we've got. The Vets at home base have positively identified the monkey in the aerial photograph as a macaque."

Tibbets tried unsuccessfully to stifle a giggle.

"A little reverence back there, mister. These boys went to school a lot of years to provide us with this information!" Bates said with feigned seriousness. "Macaques. I don't see where it makes a hoot-in-a-holler's difference what kind of monkey it is, but we're paying these guys and they took nearly three hours to come up with this, so pay attention. They also spent a Cadillac's worth of taxpayer's money on the phone to Balboa Park, the San Diego Zoo, talking to their monkey lady about these macaques. Know what they found out?"

Gerber and Tibbets shook their heads on cue.

"Macaques are *curious*! How's that for getting your money's worth? They're attracted to anything shiny, so naturally they're interested in our umbrellas."

Bates took a long drink of his coffee, then pulled a face that could have been intense pain or ecstasy.

"Damned fine coffee. You're sure this is government issue?"

"Sergeant Woodard will explain it to you if you're interested. He's a genius with grounds and big enough to go bear hunting with a switch. I'll introduce you later. So what do we do—paint the umbrellas."

"Won't work. That option went down early. Paint insulates the aluminum and cuts down on reflection. We thought about dropping poison around each site, but the public affairs boys nearly had kittens over that one. Sierra Club, EPA, all that stuff. Wish to hell they'd have said something about it to the Vets, though, 'cause they out and asked the Monkey Lady what would be a good toxin! Can't wait for that to make the papers." The colonel chuckled into his cup as he drained it. "No, the answer came down to either finding some way to permanently bolt the reflectors down—which I didn't care for since you have to be finished no later than tomorrow night and it would take too much time—and the simple approach. A Spec 4 came up with the simple approach, naturally. He's a sergeant now, by the way, and if this thing's a success I may give him a damned rocker to put under it!''

"Figures," Tibbets kibitzed.

"Yeah, don't it just?" Bates agreed.

"And the answer *is*?" Gerber asked in true game-show fashion.

"We provide the precocious simians with something even more attractive, keep the little darlings busy for a few days until we've finished what comes next, and then they can have the damned reflectors!"

"Brilliant!" Tibbets said with enthusiasm.

"And that is?" Gerber pleaded, beginning to tire of being the one to keep the conversation pointed.

"These!" Bates said, then produced a handful of familiar silver cones from his pocket.

"Well, I'll be damned," said Gerber.

"Probably," Bates agreed happily. "Especially if word of *this* gets back to the Monkey Lady in San Diego!"

"Should work," Tibbets observed.

Gerber felt a twinge of déjà vu at the pilot's words. Where had he heard that before?

THREE THOUSAND FEET BELOW, Route 9 rolled past, then opened up into a northerly fork just east of the city of Khe Sanh. Ahead lay Lang Vei proper and, just north of that, what remained of the Lang Vei Special Forces Camp that had fallen a month earlier. The distinctive shape of the camp put a lump in Gerber's throat as he thought of the friends and allies who had perished in its defense. He better than most knew what those men had felt, for A-555 had suffered a similar fate, albeit from within and while he, personally, had been outside the wire. The Bru tribesmen of Lang Vei had remained loyal to the cause, however, and had walked into Khe Sanh prepared to continue battle. But the brass hats had decided they would be a liability and had suggested evacuation to Cam Lo.

In a decision that was entirely too typical, yet one that wouldn't make the papers, General Lam, the I Corps commander, had denied the Bru aircraft to evacuate—those airlifts were for the minority in the area, the Vietnamese—and consigned the Bru to their villages to live or die as the NVA decided. At a time when human rights were all the rage in the U.S., Gerber thought, the GVN was still playing the same tribal crap that had kept them at war on some level for nearly four centuries. In the end it would likely boil down to something as elemental as Highland Vietnamese against Lowland Vietnamese, just as it had always been.

Lang Vei slipped past, leaving them suspended between the two major features of the area, Tiger Tooth Mountain to the north and Co Roc just inside the Laotian border to the southwest. Even at night these two peaks dominated the landscape and, as the prime high ground for each side's artillery spotters, helped to alter it.

"Kinda look like Mother Nature's boobs, don't they?" Tibbets suggested.

"Yeah, I guess so, if you don't take into account all that acne the B-52s have rained on her breastbone," Gerber allowed. "Mind you, one's a bit larger than the other. Kinda reminds me of a gal in high school. Let's see, her name was—"

"ADF!" Tibbets interrupted, signaling there was a song on the LF/DF he wanted to hear. "Country Joe and the Fish! This is supposed to be drivin' them nuts back in the World."

Gerber selected the ADF position on his comm panel and listened until the song went off and was replaced by a commercial message for savings bonds. "Country Joe and the who?" he asked.

"The Fish. Country Joe and the Fish. Don't tell me you haven't heard of them?"

"Can't say as I have. These new groups slay me with their names. Seems like only yesterday that every band around was named after a men's magazine or a prophylactic. We had the

Playboys, the Esquires, the Rogues, the Sultans, the Sheikhs, names like that.''

"Did you have one called the Reservoir Tips? The Pre-Lubes?'' Tibbets asked from behind his goggles.

"You know what I mean. Now it's the Stones, the Beatles, Four-F Freddie and the Bedwetters, Phil Dirt and the Bulldozers. I mean, where will it all end?''

"You're beginning to sound like a parent, you know that?''

"I guess I'm old enough to be one, if I ever find anyone I dislike enough to marry, that is. How long to our first drop?''

"I make it about ten minutes to where we left off last night. Nice of them to let us start there and work our way back, huh?'' Tibbets said.

"Yeah. Hey, check this out!'' Gerber exclaimed.

Near the American base a huge explosion sent great geysers of fire into the sky. Compared to the smaller flashes of mortars, which were commonplace both going and coming at Khe Sanh, it was impressive.

"What do you make that to be? Rocket, maybe 122 mm?''

"Maybe. Thought I saw a muzzle-flash out there just before it hit, though, so it might be one of Charlie's 130s or 152s. The briefers said there was some heavy stuff somewhere northwest of Hill 881S and to be on the lookout for it, so that might be it.''

"Can we call it in? Fix a position maybe?''

"Nope. Radio silence it is. You heard the man, Mack. Unless, of course, we get a really good fix on our way out. I've got Charlie Battery's push on a card somewhere.''

It was like flying through a lazy Fourth of July fireworks display. The sky seemed alive with flying colors as the big guns from Co Roc and Position 305 rained shell after shell down onto the Marines at Khe Sanh and the Marine batteries answered in kind. Thin green tracers arced into the camp only to pass ruby red ones on their way out. Flares from both sides dotted the sky, spewing little tails of smoke behind them along with sparks like the rocket engines on Buck Rogers's spaceship. And everywhere there were the fires set by bombs, bullets and artillery blasts.

Gerber wondered why anyone would need radar to find the target area, but quickly knew why as they flew through an acrid cloud of smoke. From forty thousand feet at night the area would look like a living thing, a mutant firefly perhaps, and picking friend from foe would be sheer guesswork.

Within minutes they were in position for the first reflector, and Gerber was surprised at how easy it was to install. They were getting good at it now, and the extra items they left behind with each reflector could be dispensed from inside the helicopter in a matter of seconds. He still wondered what people would think of this new wrinkle.

The first hour after midnight found them back at Camp Carroll for their second refueling of the night. It had gone well—all the original sites had been revisited and another reflector deployed to replace the ones the monkeys had taken. Airborne laboratories, which monitored the myriad sensors already in place in the target area, radioed confirmation of each reflector as it popped up on their screens, then fed this information into the banks of computers at the Infiltration Center at Nakhom Phanom.

From the plot on his laminated map Gerber could make out the shape of the target area they were defining as something akin to a boat. At least that was what it looked like in his mind. With each reflector successfully put in place, he rubbed its corresponding spot from the map, just in case. Had he known which points to connect he'd have come up with a maze that would provide radar coordinates for every position on the ground. Tibbets noted that this resupply stop left just two boxes of reflectors remaining until they were finished.

"And then we can take a good day's rest and fly back to Da Nang in time to hit the city, right?" Gerber suggested. "With our sleep-wake schedule we should be able to party all those nurses right under the table, huh?''

"Aren't you forgetting the other little item on our shopping list?" Tibbets asked while depressing the starter switch on his collective lever.

Gerber waited until the engine had come up to speed and ignited, a fearful-sounding operation during which the fuel control seemingly tossed a bucket of fuel into the little turbine and hoped for the best. Even after two nights of starts and stops he still jumped at the sound of the fuel igniting behind his head, and this worried him far more than Colonel Bates saying, "Oh, by the way."

"That's additional tasking to be performed should it become handy to do so, and I doubt that it will," he answered.

"Maybe. Have you ever known the brass to leave a suggestion like that lying around for long before making it an edict, though?" Tibbets asked while boosting his rpms up to operating speed, then reaching out and tapping the face of a gauge until it blinked into life.

"We'll see, Doug."

"Yeah, I guess we will at that. Something the colonel didn't consider about that deal that he should have, though. Where would a gook sit in here?" the pilot asked while picking the little helicopter up to low hover. "I mean, how could we possibly bring them back an NVA if there's only room for two in here the way we're configured?"

Gerber didn't want to think about that but did anyway, and cared less and less for each new option he considered.

13

KOMPONG RAU
CAMBODIA

The women and children were in the fields when the soldiers returned, and Lao, wanting a moment's respite before facing widows and orphans, ordered his men to clean their weapons before leaving the camp. Weapons, he thought. Of the three squads that had chanted before the fire this morning scarcely a dozen remained and half of these had no weapons. He'd have to take partial blame for that, though he wouldn't do so in public, for not insisting the men clean their M-16s before going into combat. The American weapon was lethal enough and, with its smaller ammunition, far lighter than most, but it did have a tendency to jam if not kept spotless. And the radio, he'd certainly hear about that. It should have remained in camp with the automatic weapons and extra ammo. In fact, the way things turned out they all should have!

The march back to Kompong Rau had been difficult and disorganized. Three of the men were wounded and another route had to be taken in case the enemy had found their trail and set an ambush. Each step was sheer drudgery beneath the thick canopy where the air never moved and the heat sapped the strength from muscles in short order. The humidity was such that sweat wouldn't evaporate to offer relief, and swarms of thirsty insects fed and drank from the marchers unmercifully. Now, in the relative comfort of a hootch, Lao was torn between the need to quench the thirst burning in his throat and chest and just giving in to the urge to lie down and sleep. Sleep won the battle.

Lao found several rolled-up straw mats next to the rear wall of the hootch and selected one for his bed. The only other furniture was a pair of wooden cases that had once held ammunition of some sort, mortar rounds he judged from their size, and one of these made a handy seat as he undressed. The sandals fell from his feet, releasing numerous little clay zigzags from the tire treads. With one hand he unfastened the wooden buttons of his shirt while the other tugged at the drawstring of his pants. He stood to allow the pants to fall to the floor and sought to pull the sweaty shirt away at the same time.

"Ai-eee!" he screamed as the pain shot through his chest. Then he stepped back as if to flee from an unseen attacker, tripped over the ammo case and landed flat on his back on the packed-earth floor.

During his fall he jerked the shirt free from his chest and abdomen where it had adhered to his wounds, and this would have occasioned another outburst had he not been winded on impact. He sat up and inspected the area on his breast where he'd been bitten, then followed the path of ruin down his body. The bite was easily the worst of the lot, though several of the deep scratches were bleeding again after having their scabs ripped off with the shirt. The bite did not bleed but had taken on an unusual appearance, a swollen lump with twin crescents of tooth marks like small mouths, with fine rays of orange radiating away from the lump. The scratches that weren't bleeding had mud sealed beneath their scabs, which added to the general discoloration of his lower torso.

A muted wail rose up from the paddies; the women now knew the fates of their men, Lao realized. Foolish to let soldiers bring their families with them here, he thought, another bullet for his report to General Giap. On second thought, after the major defeats suffered by the NVA over the past two months, he might be well advised to concentrate his report on the more positive aspects of his operations. It wasn't uncommon for the bearer of bad tidings to be shot and, considering the thousands already dead, another major wouldn't be missed. Lao lay back to consider what he would say in his report and made a mental list of his accomplishments that totally ignored either raid on Go Bac Chien.

He'd succeeded in mastering the Americans' radio procedures and, on the occasions when they'd managed to ambush a patrol and get their authentication codes, had been able to call in fire missions and evacuation helicopters. These had resulted in many enemy killed and their weapons taken for future use against them. As a personal project he had also sent back to America numerous walking reminders of their folly. This he considered a brainstorm that should be made policy throughout the army. The American press would gladly use these pitiful mutants to spread his message—of this he was certain—though why the American government allowed this he didn't understand. Not that anyone really understood the Americans, least of all his late father.

Lao curled up on the mat with his back to the open door, then closed his eyes against the light and his ears to the sorrowful keening in the paddies. Soon he was transported back over the years and miles to Quom Lat, the small hamlet near Vinh where he grew to boyhood. His father was a well-respected man in the village, despite his position in the government, and often entertained friends with his tales of adventure. Cho, as his father was called, had moved to the North from Quang Tri Province a few years before the Japanese invaded and was initially viewed with the suspicion normally reserved for newcomers to the village. The fact that Cho was educated and spoke excellent French and English didn't endear him, either, but did catch the ear of the local political officer who duly reported his presence up his chain of command.

Soon Cho was offered a commission in the Viet Minh to act as interpreter, and it was while serving in this capacity that he was ordered back to the South. Cho wasn't happy to leave his wife and children, but found the senior officers he was working with to be a dedicated lot and was soon caught up in the fervor known only to freedom fighters.

The commanding officer was easygoing, hardly the warrior type at all, and was also fluent in French. They would have long conversations on sweltering nights in that romantic tongue and speak of art and literature and a host of topics on which the others in their unit were ignorant. It was during one of these conversations that a sentry came in all wide-eyed and announced they had a unique visitor.

It was an American captain who had parachuted into the nearby jungle. He was a young man, this captain, but not without charm. He brought with him a collection of rare and beautiful butterflies as a gift to the commander, and the fact that he knew Ho to be a collector spoke well of his sources. He also brought an offer—the Americans sought assistance in the form of guerrilla attacks against the Japanese to deny them the use of Da Nang and other bases in their operations against the Philippines. In return for this assistance America agreed to intercede on behalf of the Viet Minh to force the French to allow local participation in the government of Vietnam.

Cho interpreted from English to Vietnamese while the American was present, then, at Ho's request, from English to French after the captain had been sent away to a meal and a bed. Ho was enthusiastic but not without his doubts. Japan was a fearsome force for the fledgling Viet Minh to take on for the convenience of another nation, and France wasn't known as a country that would listen to reason, even from powerful America.

They talked about the offer into the early morning, with Ho often asking for interpretations into the nearest equivalent of either of his languages. It was here that Cho became culpable. Often there were no literal translations from the Americanized English into either French or Vietnamese, so Cho was allowed to choose from a range of alternatives and thereby flavor Ho's understanding of what was actually being offered. In the end Ho considered the fact that France was currently occupied by the Germans and that, should the Americans lift that oppressive yoke from French shoulders, then perhaps they *would* be in position to dictate certain concessions on Vietnam's behalf. Cho cited Russia's working as an ally with the U.S. as a precedent and, near daybreak, Ho accepted the offer.

The rest was history. At the end of the war a British brigadier thanked the Vietnamese for their assistance, then demanded the return of all their weapons. Once they were disarmed he promptly returned the country to the French; the Americans remained silent. Cho was still highly thought of by Ho Chi Minh, but his counsel was seldom sought thereafter. Cho felt it was the American President who had replaced the crippled one who had reneged on the deal, and he still put forward the opinion that the U.S. held Vietnam's future.

Following the ouster of the French in 1954, this indeed seemed to be the case, for America prompted the United Nations to enter the country as a stabilizing force until elections could be held in 1956. Then more Americans were sent to prevent these elections, a puppet government was installed and the Viet Minh, indeed all South Vietnamese, found themselves again without a say in their government. Cho fell to disgrace in the eyes of the party and was forced to move back to Quang Tri "to live among those whose futures you have denied!"

Cho took along his family and worked for a time as a barber before moving to Da Nang, where he took a position as an interpreter for a shipping concern. He educated his children as best he could, then turned them over to a mission school where they received further tutoring in subjects beyond politics and languages. Cho was treated indifferently by most of the locals but shunned by those with war experience who remembered him or who maintained ties with the Viet Minh.

In 1961 the Americans came again. This time they were supposedly helping the farmers and villagers with agricultural and environmental problems at the behest of their progressive new President. In fact, they were mapping the country. These "advisers" stayed for a time in a camp near Cho's home, and Lao took to running errands for them in return for candy bars or money.

Cho was offered an enormous amount of money to act as interpreter for these huge, hairy men and he agreed. Then Cho thought of his past allegiances and tried to contact representatives of the underground forces now called the Vietcong.

The Vietcong already knew of his employment and arrived one day while Lao and his sister were in school to await his return. Cho came home for his noon meal to find his wife raped and murdered and a garrote awaiting him. All this Lao had learned later. What he remembered of that day was finding his parents mutilated and the words Thank You written in their blood on one wall. Beneath these words, as though left as a signature, was another—*America*.

Lao and his sister, Xuan, went to the mission school and told their teacher what had happened. Xuan, being younger, was offered up for adoption, and Lao was claimed by a church agency for schooling in the United States. He found himself smaller in many regards than the American boys, and the butt of their jokes. He found further that almost no one he met there even knew his country existed! When his country was mentioned in the news programs, it was invariably mispronounced and television film rarely showed cities such as Da Nang, just simple farmers tending water buffalo or women in rice paddies. The corrupt puppet government gave way to yet another when the Americans' supposedly, saintlike President authorized the assassination of its leader, Ngo Dinh Diem, yet nothing really changed.

After four years he knew he had to go home, had to do something to avenge his father's death and regain respect for his ancestral name. His English was now accentless, owing to many hours of practice to avoid being teased by smart-aleck upper classmen, and he had two years of engineering studies to offer along with a heart full of hate for everything American. The North Vietnamese accepted it all.

Lao awoke in darkness to the sound of heavy rain pouring down on the thatched roof. The rain drowned out any sobs or sniffs that may have still come from the other hootches, a blessing he didn't bother counting at the moment since he was still caught up with the past. He hardly noticed that he was alone—no young *co* to keep him warm tonight, but then he really didn't need one for that purpose since a mild fever was currently taking care of that quite nicely. As he drifted back into sleep, his thoughts were divided between his progress in regaining the prominence of his family name in the eyes of his superiors and the need to start back north the next day. Surely, he thought, his operations down here would get his name mentioned favorably, and that was a prerequisite for promotion.

"They'll remember my name," he mumbled through dry lips to the wet night. "They'll all remember my name!"

14

CAMP A-555

"Lao. His name is—or at least *was*—Nguyen Bei Lao," Kit said softly, reluctantly. "I thought I recognized his voice on the tapes, but it was so long ago and we have grown so much that I . . ."

Fetterman sought her eyes as her voice trailed off to silence, but was denied them as she bowed her head, lowering a curtain of blue-black hair around her face. Maxwell's trained gaze measured the response to her words on the face of the NVA soldier and found in the man's twisted misery that Kit spoke the truth. Now he would have to consider what advantage this information would afford him, that and how far he should trust his converted scout in this matter. He was dying to ask in what capacity she'd known this Lao, even to the point of allowing himself the briefest instant of erotic curiosity, before the years of training rose to the forefront.

"His rank?" he asked evenly.

"I should think major by now, perhaps even colonel."

"Minh?" Maxwell said in a voice that rang in the confined space and elicited cringes from both prisoners.

Minh pivoted the NVA around to face him, then drew back one booted foot as though to kick the man ostensibly on or near his wound.

"Major! He is maa-jor!" the man screamed while trying to hop away from Minh.

"Very good. I have just a few more questions and then I'll send for Sergeant Washington and his medical kit. Tony, how about escorting Kit here over to her hootch where she can rest. Stay with her, if you don't mind, and I'll be along directly," Maxwell said in a gentle voice that effectively masked his rising excitement and annoyed him. He wanted the prisoners to remain on edge, insecure, and in fear of more pain until he'd finished interrogating them, and the last thing he wanted was to sound fatherly. "Minh will stay, along with Sergeant Krung. And would you please send in Stonehand? Now, let's get with it!"

Fetterman shouldered his own weapon, lifted Kit's carbine from where she'd leaned it against the wall and used it to push open the door. She raised her head slightly to look up at him as she stepped past him, her hair falling back to the sides of her oval face to reveal eyes filled with confusion and just a twinge of defiance. He knew as well as she what Maxwell's seemingly good-natured request for him to escort her to her quarters implied—that he was to remain with her until it was her turn for interrogation.

Fetterman fell into step a short distance behind her and remained there, not so much to cover her with a weapon as to admire the smooth grace of her walk. Kit's fatigues, he reflected, fit her every bit as well as Maxwell's didn't. It was of passing interest to him that he didn't find himself picturing her nude before him, but rather wondering how she would look in an *ao dai*. When they arrived at her hootch, she swung its door open wide and stepped aside for Fetterman to enter first.

"*Après vous, s'il vous plaît,*" she said, then smiled.

"*Merci,*" he answered with a slight bow, then stepped through the door, wondering what would come next and hoping it wouldn't be more French.

It wasn't. Once inside she strode purposefully to the nearest cot and began unlacing her boots. A careful inventory of her toes and the area in between followed, something Fetterman appreciated as a soldier but found almost vulgar when performed by an attractive female. Satisfied with her feet, Kit sat up and began to run the splayed fingers of each hand through her hair in an effort to comb it away from her face and down her back. The resultant hairdo left the tips of her small ears sticking up through her hair in a manner that reminded Fetterman of Mighty Mouse's girlfriend. Next she unbuttoned the top button of her fatigue shirt, a move that caused him to forget cartoon mice and wonder if the French influence was about to exert itself in earnest!

"Would you like—" she began while pulling her hand from her blouse slowly "—a smoke?"

Fetterman swallowed the lump that had mysteriously risen in his throat, and declined with a shake of his head. Inside pockets, he thought. He had them on some of his own shirts, the ones he wore while in garrison. They were handy, since they allowed one to carry things in the shirt pocket without having an unprofessional unbuttoned pocket flap to worry about. Kit smoothed one of her thin black cigars into a semblance of straightness, then began patting her pockets in search of a light. With a practiced motion he produced a battered Zippo and flicked it into life.

"Thank you. I didn't know you smoked," she said, then leaned forward to bring the cigar into the flame.

"I don't. Gave it up several years ago. The lighter was a gift."

Her hand found his own as she steadied the flame under the cigar's tip and quickly lit the cigar. She didn't release his hand immediately, a fact he found both curious and confusing, until she spoke through a bluish veil of cigar smoke. "You don't trust me either, do you?"

It was a statement rather than a question and one Fetterman couldn't really answer. She'd proved herself faithful enough during previous missions, a fact made more commendable, considering where those missions had been. But why had she remained silent on this one for so long and, more importantly, why did she choose to speak out only when Maxwell was about to interrogate the NVA prisoner? More to the point, did she really think doing so would spare the man his interrogation?

"I didn't *have* to say anything at all, you know," she said. "I did so to save time that would have been wasted getting the name out of that soldier. Oh, I know Jerry Maxwell will hear all this man can say. Of course I know this! Did you think he gave me this job just on my word?"

Fetterman noticed the wick on his lighter was beginning to spark and that Kit's hand had taken on a clawlike character. He flicked the lid shut and pulled his hand free to restow the lighter in his pocket. It was hot against the flesh of his thigh, even through the sweat-drenched cloth of his fatigues. The feeling reminded him of interrogation sessions witnessed and those rumored, including those administered by the CIA, of which Kit no doubt had firsthand knowledge.

"Then why?" he wanted to know.

"Why what? Why did I tell? Or why didn't I tell when I heard the tapes?"

"Either. Both!"

"Because I wasn't sure it was his voice. No, I think I didn't want it to be his voice. We were children together for several years, though were it not for his father we would not have been friends. Boy children are brought up differently from girl children in my... my childhood home."

Fetterman nodded understandingly, relatively certain she had almost said my *country* and unsure how much emphasis he should put on that, since she'd grown up in North Vietnam.

"Girl children go to school like boys, though it was not always so, but only so far and then they return to the fields or their family's work. My father, as you know, was French, and my mother taught me what she knew of that language. When Lao came to live in our village, it was wonderful because his father had taught him languages also. It was from his father that I learned my English and to read the good books he brought. Lao's father treated me as his own and made me an eager student—he knew so much of a world that others denied existed. I asked him once why it was that our political teacher claimed the Americans and Europeans were starving, yet in the next session spoke of how they all drove automobiles and wasted their considerable fortunes on decadent behavior?"

Kit smiled as she remembered, then sat back on the bed with her heels pulled up next to her buttocks and her arms around her knees. It wasn't hard for Fetterman to imagine her as a bright-eyed child not long ago, tormenting her mentor with irrefutable child logic.

"I said, 'Uncle Cho, if they have so many automobiles, then why do they not trade one for food?' I pictured roads lined with automobiles, each with a skeleton for a chauffeur. It made no sense to me then. Lao called me a fool for asking, but his father was glad I was curious. He said curiosity was better than a full stomach and a thirst for answers better than a full well. He never did tell me why hungry people drove automobiles, though, and I think that's when I started questioning what I was being taught to accept on faith."

"Makes sense. Lao went on believing, though. Right?"

"I don't know. He was a good friend and a very good person until we were in our teenage years, then he changed. He did not grow as fast as the other boys, and they took to teasing him about his size. Cho told him to ignore them or to think of them as only poor ignorant farm children, which of course they were, and to believe in himself. Lao was smart, a quick study with languages and history and a genius in math. He was a natural for higher education, and for a while he seemed to be happy with this. Or so we thought."

Kit stubbed out her cigar in a makeshift ashtray fashioned from a C-rations can. Fetterman noted that the can had held lima beans and ham and wondered idly if the ashes might not have helped the taste had the can still had been full.

"Then what happened?" he asked, partly because he was genuinely interested and partly to cover the sound of his intestines growling—he needed to eat something in the worst way if lima beans and ham could put his digestive tract in gear!

"Then the other boys' voices started to deepen, and Lao's did not. Other things about them changed also, while he remained the same, and he became bitter. I must confess, I teased him at times myself, but it was only because everyone else did and I thought it was expected of me. He reacted with violence. At first he would take his anger out on small animals, sometimes torturing a young bird or civet cat for hours until it died. He fashioned snares and traps of all sorts to capture or hurt animals, too. Then he took to picking on the smaller boys and some of us girls. I was a favorite target, since his father liked me so much. He would pinch us, pull our hair and sometimes twist our arms until they were almost broken—and he laughed all the time he was doing it."

Kit's eyes looked into the distant past, and an expression of extreme distaste contorted her features as she summoned the next memory into her conscious. "Then he raped a young girl and threatened to kill her if she told anyone, but I knew. I did not tell anyone for a time, and then he attacked her again."

She paused to pull out another cigar and, before Fetterman could reach his Zippo, lit it with a paper match. A thin stream of smoke escaped her lips and sped its way toward the ceiling, and when she resumed talking, her voice was lower and more coarse, menacing. "This time Lao hurt her. He struck her in the eye with a rock as she tried to get free of him, and it bled badly. The more she struggled the crazier he became until he wasn't Lao anymore, but an animal. He bit her breast until it bled and slapped her face until it was swollen. When he was finished with her, he again swore to kill her if she told anyone—told her to say she'd been trampled by one of the water buffalo or had fallen from a tree.''

"This time I couldn't keep quiet. He had been making remarks about me around the other boys, about how I was coming between his father and himself and about how girls should keep in their place. He also started referring to me as a bastard, a *French* bastard, and I was afraid of him. I started to tell his father about the attacks, but his father suddenly didn't want to talk to me! I thought Lao had been telling Cho lies to turn him against me, but that wasn't the case. Cho was in trouble with his superiors. I told my brother about Lao, and he promised to attend to him, but when he went to wait for Lao to come out of his house, he found they had both fled. I next saw Lao two years ago. He had returned and was an officer in the army. Fortunately he didn't see me then and, until I heard his voice on Maxwell's tape machine, I had no idea he was working in the South.''

They sat in silence for a while, Kit with eyes closed and chin propped on her knees and Fetterman staring up through the blue haze of smoke at a weak timber that was beginning to sag under the weight of its sandbags. How often had he lain awake after a night patrol or recce trying to will himself to sleep while subconsciously noting the material condition of every board and bag.

The NVA soldier had cried out a few times during Kit's story, a sound fully expected by both of them and little noted by either, but now he'd gone quiet. Fetterman assumed Maxwell had what he wanted from the man and had sent T. J. Washington with his soothing needle to his belated relief. Kit would be next. The thought rankled at Fetterman's nerves, although he knew well enough that it had to be if she were to continue on this mission—or did it?

"I believe you," he said sincerely, and did.

Kit lifted her chin slightly and smiled, then said, "Thank you, Sergeant Tony. Now maybe you will see why I want to kill Lao—myself.''

"ONE QUESTION, KIT," Maxwell began with an obvious lie. "Is it true that the Vietcong killed Lao's parents?"

Kit thought about her answer for a time while carefully surveying the CIA man. His clothes were almost comical in their fit and did nothing to disguise the fact that he wasn't a soldier. The session with the NVA had been relatively brief, so she assumed the man had either told all he knew quickly or else had lapsed into a coma from his pain. The session wasn't totally one-sided in its misery, though. Dark crescents of perspiration were evident where Maxwell's armpits likely resided in his uniform, and his face was even redder than before.

"It is rumored so. A hasty mistake, or so it was claimed. The regime in the North changes from time to time, and those in favor one day may find themselves out the next. Lao was fortunate to return when his father's memory was favorable to those in power, or their guilt was heavy. Either way it gained him an appointment to officer rank."

"So, it *could* be true, then," Maxwell asked in his lawyer's voice as though he wanted a definite yes or no to his question before he continued. He did.

"Yes. It could be true and, as I said, is rumored to be so. Why do you ask?"

"No reason," Maxwell lied again, and convinced no one. "Get a bite to eat and then we'll meet at the staging area. Word is Major Lao is planning to return to the North soon, so we're stepping up this operation. That's all."

Kit took her dismissal at face value, though not without a measure of curiosity. His last sentence had seemed the biggest lie of all, and yet, when she stood and started for the door, he made no move to stop her. Fetterman lifted her carbine hesitantly, then, after getting a small nod of approval from Maxwell, handed it to her.

The air outside felt cooler than she remembered it, and the fading sun sent the long shadow of the fire control tower almost to the edge of the camp. She felt the light-headedness of the recently released for a second and then felt the indescribable weight of human eyes on her back. She knew without looking that it would be Sergeant Krung. Krung was the logical choice, but then she and Krung had something in common few in the camp could understand, least of all the Americans.

15

THE WESTERN SLOPE OF
CO ROC, LAOS

"Not tonight we don't!" Tibbets vowed sincerely.

As they crept up the side of the mountain, Gerber watched through his night vision goggles, and suddenly realized the goggles weren't really needed. From a point halfway up Co Roc's northern face, all the way to its peak, there was a constant stream of outgoing artillery fire. The amount of light produced by it caused Gerber to wonder if perhaps they were in danger of discovery.

"I see what you mean. I doubt anyone will want to fly through that anytime soon. Do you think there's a chance they could spot us?"

"I doubt it. Looking down into the valley, we blend in pretty well as long as we stay low. You sure you don't want to just drop an umbrella here and be done with it?" the pilot asked, the hope evident in his voice even over the crackle of static.

"Too far off and too easy to spot from up here. H-hour is a day away, and they'd have plenty of time to find it. Chances are they've already spotted a flash or two in the jungle north of here but wrote them off as water in bomb craters catching the sun or something. You certain they can't hear us?"

Tibbets turned his alien face toward the Special Forces captain and waited for his goggles to focus. Gerber looked every bit as otherworldly as he, so there was no chance to discern anything from his expression.

"Well, I'll put it to you this way, Mack. If artillery dudes were all we were trying to sneak up on, we could have saved a helluva lot of Uncle Sugar's money, 'cause I doubt any of them can hear themselves break wind after two weeks in that business!"

That made sense, but didn't rule out the odd new arrival at Co Roc who might still have normal hearing—a fact Gerber was quick to point out, along with the direction to the next drop point. En route back toward the border he wondered idly what his master sergeant might be up to at this moment. It was to have been something of a busman's holiday for them both, going back to their old camp while its CO and first sergeant traveled to Nha Trang for a week of briefings and brainstorming. Now here he was in a supposedly neutral country distributing some unlikely wares in an unorthodox manner from an even more unorthodox machine. Tony was likely sacked out in his old rack, listening to the night calls of birds, while *he* prepared to dismount the tiny helicopter and could hear only the muffled hiss of rotor blades and . . . *bugles!*

At first he wasn't sure, but after dropping an additional five feet down the rope he heard them clearly. One seemed to come from directly beneath the tall teak they'd selected as a drop site and others, more muted and faint, were answering. Allowing for more that he couldn't hear, Gerber reckoned there were at least a couple of battalions below and, judging from the incessant bugling, they were ready for action. Here he found himself in a dilemma. Suspended as he was beneath the helicopter, it would be extremely difficult to climb back up without jettisoning the reflector, yet to do so would probably draw fire immediately and would definitely compromise all the hard work of the past two nights. They only way out was up.

The three arms spans it took to bring him chin-to-skid with the helicopter were accompanied by much flailing as his awkward load took the rotor's downblast and converted it to drag. Worse, it threatened to set him to twirling, which would foul his ropes and necessitate a spin in the opposite direction to straighten them.

Gerber hooked his chin over the thin metal tube that was the skid and took a couple of quick turns of the rope through the carabiner clip on his harness to lock himself in position, then fought against the vicious wind to grasp the reflector tight enough to shove it back inside the cockpit. Tibbets's face appeared briefly in the door, an eerie sight in the dull red glow of the subdued instrument panel, then disappeared again as he took up his vigil of the distant horizon to hold their hover steady. Despite Tibbets's efforts the little helicopter wobbled slightly as Gerber sought a better grip before ridding himself of the now-fluttering reflector, and then the chopper gave a sideways lurch that caught them both by surprise.

Gerber reacted as a man always will when something to which he is clinging threatens to leave without him: he dropped all else and clung to the skid with both hands. Tibbets righted the craft quickly but felt the inevitable sag as he swapped lift for directional control. To counter their slight descent, he pulled up on the collective lever gently while neutralizing the added torque with the foot pedals, a process that took less time to put into action than it did to recognize the need for it.

Gerber felt the drop in the pit of his stomach and instinctively pressed his legs together and bent his knees—the standard reflex of anyone who routinely parachutes. His boot brushed against the top of the teak, then as quickly rose above it. There was a tug at the carabiner clip, which grew to a steady pull as the helicopter crept higher, and then it became pain.

In the cockpit Tibbets felt the presence of the tree, felt it in every hair follicle on the nape of his neck, but maintained his discipline and with it his smooth touch on the controls. It would have been all too easy to merely haul back on the collective and power the ship up and away from trouble, all too easy and entirely too noisy. His hair began to unbristle as he felt the ship start back up, ever so slowly, only to fray out anew when it stopped rising and started to keel over to one side as though anchored.

The harness continued to tighten around Gerber's chest as the helicopter pulled the tangled ropes ever tighter. The rope made a crisp snapping sound as one round pulled itself off the top of another on the clip and the squeeze became like that of a boa constrictor. Any thought he may have had of shouting to the pilot to slack off died as what wind he had left came out in a spurt when the rope popped taut. The upper limbs of the teak were now pulled upward to display the tangle of nylon rope caught in its branches like so much spiderweb in a head of hair. The branches would give, then snap back, the rope would stretch, then reclaim its natural length, and on the occasions when both limbs and rope were contracting, Gerber felt certain the next sound he heard would be either ribs or harness breaking.

It was natural enough to look toward the impedance, and Doug Tibbets wasted no time in doing so. To his surprise he saw the curved surface of Gerber's helmet just under the door. What, then, was holding them? The helicopter was getting restless at the elastic nature of its tether and beginning to react violently to the tugs and eases. The timing of these was such that by the time Tibbets got one correction in, the other condition appeared to aggravate an already deteriorating situation. The corrections were getting larger and more rapid, the helicopter was beginning to make excessive noise, and he could only imagine what anyone nearby would think of the ruckus being raised in the treetops. The only thing to do was to try to pull free and flee. Tibbets tightened his grip and prepared to pull an armload of collective pitch the next time there was slack.

Gerber weighed his options superficially, the will to survive coming to the fore with booming voice to dictate his course of action. Foresaking his purchase on the skid with one hand and trusting the chrome-moly carabiner clip perhaps more than its present state would justify, he reached for the sheathed knife on his shoulder strap. One swipe of the Ironmonger blade sent the rope unraveling into the darkness below just as the first yellowish-green tracers came bouncing and boiling up through the foliage. There was a second while he turned his face upward to be force-fed air from the laboring blades that he didn't fully appreciate the new colors in his night, then re-alization yanked him back to reality at about the same time Tibbets yanked the collective lever. The rotor blades coned upward as they jerked the small ship skyward like a homesick angel. Gerber nearly lost his boots in the process; Tibbets his lunch.

The tracers continued to fight their way through the thick jungle canopy and initially came close enough for Gerber to appreciate something Doug had said earlier about viewing them from on high. They appeared huge, like glowing tennis balls, and almost as inoffensive since they seemed to just crawl upward, growing slightly larger and more symmetrical all the time until, at the last instant, they went past. Then they would accelerate to a verdant blur that left an angry hot streak across the night. Doug had perhaps hit upon the perfect description when he'd likened them to "about what June bugs look like to motorcyclists."

After what seemed much longer than the five-minute flight it was, they were back inside Vietnam and at a short hover in a rice paddy. Gerber chiseled his hands and legs free from the skid and crawled back into the cockpit. To his relief he found the remnants of the reflector still lashed to his side, inverted, shredded and bent seven ways from Sunday, but still ac-counted for. Tibbets waited patiently while his passenger strapped in and plugged into the ICS cord, then he took off, heading due east. It was several minutes before either of them spoke.

"Didn't get it installed, huh?" Tibbets said in a laconic drawl that almost achieved the level of nonchalance he'd hoped for.

"Nope. I don't think this unit is up to snuff, anyway. Looks defective to me. How about you? You get your stuff dropped?" Gerber asked evenly as though inquiring about the weather.

"Sure did!" Tibbets declared, then broke into a broad grin.

"You *didn't*!"

"Bet your sweet ass I *did*!" he said, then rotated his head from side to side while chuckling. "Wouldn't you just love to be a crab on the crotch of the gook S-2 that gets to brief this one?"

"Bet your sweet ass I would!" Gerber agreed. Then he laughed as hard as his sore sides would let him before adding, "What say we pull in for a pit stop? I've got this sudden urge to go to the latrine."

"Me, too, if I haven't already gone. I'm afraid to check. Guess you'll be taking inventory, hmm?"

"Oh, I think everything's still attached. Causing too much pain to be anywhere else. But speaking of inventory, I *will* need another harness."

"And a new rope?"

"And a new rope."

As the lights of Camp Carroll filled the windshield, Gerber massaged his chest and again wondered what his running mate back at A-555 was doing at this moment. He reasoned a beer or two was making its way through Fetterman's sleeping carcass and envied him that. The thought of beer caused his bladder to pulse and made the last five minutes of the flight seem almost as long as the ones spent clutching the skid—almost.

"YES, FATHER. I have read my lesson," Lao muttered in a small voice, dreaming. "You would like to discuss it *now*? Surely you tire of going over each one twice, Father. Or is Colonel Beng visiting today to hear our lessons? Is that why? I read it well, just as you have taught me, Father, and I know it all. I'll not embarrass you, Father. I'd never embarrass you!"

Lao's last protestation came out in a boyish whine that threatened tears and caused him to stir. Even with his eyes open his surroundings seemed dreamlike, with all edges softened by the bluish light that streamed in through the open door. This, he thought, was just a continuation of the dream, another chapter, another scene, one he might want to sit up to view. Sitting up seemed a logical thing to do since his straw mat was soaked, but on trying to rise he felt the real author of his discomfort. A stab of pain shot through his chest and ribs as he leaned forward at the waist, bringing a choked cry to his throat. His hands sought the source of the pain and found his chest covered with clammy sweat. By rolling onto his side first, he managed to struggle to his knees and then stand upright without undue pain, but the fever made keeping his balance difficult. His rifle made for a steadying cane as he worked his way to the door and into the bright moonlight to lean against the doorframe. He was content to stand there in the nude and let the night air wash over his body, to feel the timid breeze evaporate some of his sweat and cool him. There remained, however, a central area that wouldn't be cooled. Cautiously he traced this area with the fingertips of one hand.

The area around the bite wound was swollen to a hard mound that burned like a hot coal, making anything but a shallow breath extremely painful. Farther down, the deeper scratch wounds rose atop smaller lumps, and some of these oozed a greenish pus that in the moonlight looked black. Lao's eyes reluctantly followed his hand's progress and registered the purple rays that radiated out from the more severe wounds. *Infection!* his fevered brain told him as another white-hot bolt

of pain surged through his slight frame in a shudder. Any fear
he might have felt was dampened by disgust as his eyes moved
down the trail of ruin that was his abdomen to his penis.

It seemed to mock him, a tiny thing—hardly worth the pain
he'd endured to protect it—and paramount among the things
that had stopped growing in his youth. It was this, in fact, that
had tempted him to kill the girl in the village, the one who'd
come upon him beside the creek. How she'd laughed upon
seeing him, laughed and pointed! The musty sleep-taste in his
mouth turned bitter as he remembered the girl's laughter and
how she'd parodied him with her thumb and index finger
brought together to almost touch. How he'd hated her for that,
the tears of shame and anger welling up in his eyes until they
overflowed and burned his reddened cheeks.

The monkeys and birds of the jungle had taken up her
laughter and amplified it with peals of their own until the entire world around him seemed to be jeering him, but they had
paid for their mirth. He'd made certain of that by hearing a
good number of them issue their last breath voicing agony instead of laughter.

The girl had paid, too, though not enough to his reckoning,
not enough by half. She, who was the wellspring of his misery, still walked the earth somewhere, though without her
virtue. If, indeed, virtue could be said to inhabit one of such
lowly birth. It hadn't helped his battered ego to find that, even
at a year younger than himself, she was already more of a
woman than he was a man.

The burning sensation in his torso drifted downward as he
recalled lying in wait for her beside the path and pulling her
into the thick underbrush as she came by. She hadn't shown
fear at first, as though he were nothing to be taken seriously,
and this had enraged him. With the rage had come an excitement he hadn't experienced before. This excitement had
surged as he'd ripped away her loose-fitting top to reveal
smallish, cone-shaped breasts with impertinent nipples the
color of coffee. That she should have developed so far had in-

furiated him further, as had the fact that she had a fine wisp of pubic hair while he was still as bare as a babe.

Her breasts had haunted him, taunted him, even after he had raped her and sent her in tears back to the village with the promise of worse should she tell anyone. She hadn't told, but the thought of her wouldn't let him rest. The next time he had attacked her he had tried to cleave the nipple from one breast with his teeth, to disfigure her as nature had chosen to disfigure him. The memory of biting her brought a fresh twinge of pain from his own chest and broke his train of thought.

"So," he said softly to the lightening morning, "*this* is what it felt like!"

And he was glad. A cough from a nearby hootch sent him back from the door to get dressed before anyone saw him, though he knew they dared not laugh at him now. No one laughed at him now, no one who lived to tell about it, and least of all young girls. Yes, they'd paid for that indiscretion and would continue to pay until he rose high enough in rank to have access to the sources he'd need to locate the original girl who'd started it all. Then he would put paid to her for good. But that, he realized, was for the future. Now he needed something to break his fever and antibiotics to fight the infection, and that meant access to medical supplies.

There were antibiotics to be had at the larger base camps, mostly black market supplies that had entered the country from American and United Nations organizations and that had been misrouted by greedy and/or sympathetic officials in the South. Capitalism in action, he thought with a snide grin. But these supplies were often adulterated, old or spoiled due to lack of refrigeration during their transport. What he required was fresh antibiotics and dressings, the type to be found aboard the American Medevac helicopters, along with enough morphine to dull the pain while he returned to the North. He grabbed his rifle and started to don his backpack, then decided its straps would be too painful. Instead, he took the two grenades from it and tucked their spoons under his web belt on either side of the empty knife scabbard.

He stared at the empty scabbard for a moment, remembering the girl at Go Bac Chien along with the other girl whose face he'd mentally fixed upon her as he'd driven the knife home. Someone else will have to give up their knife, he thought, but only for a short time since the Americans had plenty of knives and there would soon be enough for all.

"And I'll save a special one for *you* Brouchard Bien Soo Ta Emilie, wherever you are," he said out loud, leaving the dark mask of hatred on his face as he went out to rouse his troops.

16

THE PARROT'S BEAK

"The Sneaky Petes from Tay Ninh West just reported in," Ben Willow said over the ICS to Fetterman. "They had some light traffic along the Trail during the night and managed to thump a few of them, but it was just supply bikes and all headed south."

"Check. Our boy is keeping to the Cambodia side if he's smart, and if he's heading back north. Damn! We'll have to make sure. We'll have to get more units along the trail, that's all," Fetterman answered, having to stop himself short of saying they'd need to alert units to the north that their quarry was headed their way, realizing that wasn't an option.

Their helicopter turned to reverse its course along a lazy racetrack pattern running north-south along the border. The morning sun was framed in the open door and hung there in the pale eastern sky like an over-easy egg. The soldiers on the sunny side yawned deeply and sneezed in response to the sun, yet enjoyed their turn to bask in its heat and let the dawn dampness be drawn from their fatigues. Fetterman likened them to turtles on a log, the steel pots of his troops like so many mudslider shells and the olive drab flight helmets of the crew perched atop thin necks like snappers. He peeled back the camouflage strip to consult his watch and found they had been airborne for over an hour this trip.

"How long until we need fuel?" he asked the Peter Pilot.

"Oh, we can put down anytime you like, Master Sergeant. Or we can stay out another, what? Forty-five minutes?" the lanky warrant officer said to his pilot-in-command as much as to Fetterman.

"About that, I suppose," the command pilot, a freckle-faced youth in his late teens, agreed. "Unless you want to go down and take a look around, then we can zip back for a top-off of motion lotion and come back to get you. Your choice."

Fetterman considered this. It would feel good to get out and stretch his legs, maybe run through a rehearsal of the ambush they'd planned should they locate their target. It would be good training and give him a chance to see what Willow could do in the way of tracking. He looked around at the faces of his soldiers, his eyes coming to rest on Kit's sleeping face. It was a nice face, even while covered in smears and streaks of camouflage as it was now—an innocent face, not at all the same face he'd seen the night before. Then she'd had the face of a wounded animal—part anguish, part danger.

"That sounds good. How long do you estimate your turn-around?"

"Depends on where you want out, but I think thirty mikes should cover it. Mr. Davies and I are flying the next lift, so we won't need to turn over," the teenager said in a voice devoid of youth.

Fetterman leaned forward to accept the acetate-covered map from the Peter Pilot along with a grease pencil. The pilot's finger indicated their present position, then went to his radio panel to reselect the ADF in time to hear a manic voice pour through the static. "Goooooooooooooood morning, Vietnam!" the voice brayed, bringing a smile to the pilot's lips, which were soon working silently as he sang along with a rock tune. Fetterman chose a spot on the map where the Vaico Oriental looped its muddy way south. The mud flats alongside the river

would betray any recent movement of troops through the area
and the thick growth alongside it would provide cover should
they make contact and need to escape.

"Here," he said, indicating the site on the river.

The Peter Pilot took the map back to show it to his younger
senior, who nodded and banked the helicopter into the sun
before starting a descent. The drop brought sleeping eyes wide
open and allowed Fetterman a chance to brief his people with
shouts and sign language before they arrived. A pass over the
area revealed unmarred mud flats along both banks. The flats
ran up to the edge of a tight ribbon of jungle before giving way
to the marshy scrub of the plain.

Fetterman gave a thumbs-up to the pilot, then unlocked his
seat belt in preparation to deplane. The helicopter's flare
pressed him down in his seat as it slowed, then stopped, then
eased to the ground to rock gently before settling. As the soldiers fanned out and melted into the jungle, the helicopter was
already lifting, swinging around in a tight pedal turn and dip-
ping its nose to run back out the way it had come. As a precaution, the chopper executed mock landings in several other
open areas nearby to confuse any ears that might be listening.

The soldiers lay silent until the sound of retreating rotor
blades were gone and the normal sounds of the jungle had
resumed. The earth here was moist and smelled like a com-
post heap. And in a way it was, since the lush plant life lived
off the rot of its previous generation, which decomposed rapidly in the pressure-cooker atmosphere beneath the canopy.

Fetterman rose to one knee and surveyed the area around
him, noting the positions of his men, and *women*, he con-
sciously added. They were alternating their attention between scanning the jungle and himself. Silently he raised one
finger and circled it with a finger of his other hand. Equally
silently they moved toward him. He pointed to Krung and
Willow, then indicated they were to move ahead of the rest,
toward the river. The stealth of both men spoke well of their
training, though in Willow's case it was training in the moun-

tains of North Carolina in search of squirrel and deer rather than humans.

The soft ground made quiet movement through the jungle swift and easy. When they arrived at the juncture of jungle and riverbank, a soggy peninsula between two wide mud flats, they found a well-worn trail that paralleled the stream. Krung and Willow had taken up positions alongside the trail where they could cover it in both directions.

Fetterman was satisfied with this as a rehearsal site, but first wanted to put out pickets and scout the area. He motioned to Krung and Kit to go downriver, to Willow to accompany him up the trail, and to the others to fan out and remain in place. They'd gone a mere fifty meters up the trail when Willow's arm shot up in a closed fist. Fetterman stopped dead in his tracks, then squatted in the underbrush and readied his weapon. His ears strained to detect movement ahead but found only the normal sounds of wildlife and the muffled gurgle of the river. Willow remained standing upright alongside the trail, his fist clenched tight over his head.

Fetterman approached slowly until he was within three paces of the Indian, who still stood stiffly like a bird dog on point. There was nothing visible or audible on the trail ahead that Fetterman could see that would warrant attention. With a backward glance to confirm the master sergeant's presence, Willow lowered his arm while pointing with his rifle to something on the river side of the trail not ten feet away. Again Fetterman strained to see what Willow was concerned about and again found nothing unusual. A snake, he assumed, or maybe one of the five-pound rats that looked so much like opossums and had tempers like badgers.

"Trip wire," Willow said in hushed tones, then indicated the area again.

"Where?"

"Over there in the grass. You can't see it."

Fetterman had to agree with that, but felt a bit slighted just the same.

"Why not? You obviously did."

"No, I didn't. I heard it. An animal went through there toward the river, and I heard a twang. It's there all right, and maybe on this side of the trail, too," Willow said, then dropped to hands and knees to crawl cautiously forward.

Fetterman remained where he was, studying the ground around him while poised to spring into the underbrush should the need arise. Willow's hand moved through the air above the grass patiently until it settled on the ground, then he would leave it in place and crawl a half pace forward before beginning the procedure anew with the other hand. Three paces into the grass, his hand sprang back as though he'd touched something hot. He looked back to Fetterman and nodded him forward.

"There she is, tight as a banjo string. Something heavy on the other end I'd say, or else it's been here a while," the Indian said calmly.

"Well, let's find it." Fetterman stared down at the thin wire, which, even up close, was all but invisible against the rust-colored dirt beneath the grass.

The wire terminated at a point where the trail took a sharp turn away from the river. It was hooked into the trigger of a particularly vicious device called a Malayan Swing, a sort of huge flyswatter affair made from thick bamboo that had sharp spikes embedded in its flat surface. The graying of the cut edges on the bamboo indicated that it had, indeed, been in place for some time, and its placement indicated that whoever had set it knew something of American movement along trails. They surveyed the area around the trap and found clusters of punji sticks hidden in the clumps of brush where men would most likely take cover once the main trap had been sprung.

"Well, shall we trip it and see what it does?" Fetterman suggested.

"Better yet, why don't we move the trip wire? Charlie knows where he put this thing and, from the looks of that trail, he

knows he can walk through here as long as he keeps to the path.
Might get a couple at night.''

"Why not?" Fetterman had a new respect for this bespec-
tacled young man who still looked like an accountant. The
sweep of the Malayan Swing was set to cover the trail and the
area immediately alongside it, where the Americans would be.
A simple rerouting of the wire to run down the center of the
trail optimized the chances of its being tripped while removing it from friendly traffic.

This accomplished, they ventured an additional hundred
meters up the trail before returning to stage the rehearsal.
Fetterman briefly went through everyone's duties as had been
outlined in detail the night before and set a time limit of five
minutes for everything to be done. With a minute to spare his
troops had spread out and set the mechanical ambush that was
to be the heart of the plan and taken up their positions around
the end of the "funnel" through which the enemy would be
channeled. They even took great pains to point their weapons
low in front of them to indicate they were to merely wound the
enemy, not to kill them outright unless it became absolutely
necessary.

Fetterman simulated rigging the Fulton Extraction Unit in
a clearing along the trail and registered the disdain on Krung's
face at the very idea of allowing this enemy to survive the ambush. Kit watched impassively, though she did manage a small
smile when Fetterman mimed feeding the balloon up through
an opening in the jungle canopy.

Krung was draining the last swallow of water from his canteen to wash down his LRRP ration when he heard the
thumping rotor blades of the approaching helicopter. The
water was warm but satisfying, and as it joined the concentrated freeze-dried mixture in his stomach, it slowly swelled
to a solid lump that made him feel lazy and bloated. The helicopter grew from a pinpoint above the horizon into the drab
green tadpole shape that had become as familiar in the skies

of his country as the flocks of sea gulls that were everywhere. He still wondered what made them fly.

The old chieftain back in his mountain home, a man widely recognized as being seldom right but never in doubt, had postulated that "the big wheel on top picks it up, and the little one on back pushes it along." But Krung was almost certain this wasn't the case. Still, it *was* curious, but then so much of what these people did was curious. This operation, though, seemed the ultimate contradiction: ambush the men responsible for murdering so many in the area—a number of Americans among the victims—yet do all possible to avoid killing them! Compared to this the helicopter settling tail first onto the mud nearby was no mystery at all.

Fetterman waited until the helicopter was beginning to level its skids for touchdown before starting at a gentle lope across the open area to get on board. As he neared the whirling rotor blade and started to stoop, he saw the Peter Pilot waving frantically for them to hurry and felt his heart leap into his throat. Were they taking fire? All he could hear was the popping of the blades and the shrill whine of the turbine. He panned from side to side as he ran to see if any telltale plops of mud were kicking up that would indicate small-arms fire, but the mud was unblemished. He dived into the helicopter and quickly scrambled to the farthest seat to clear the way for the others. Within fifteen seconds they were aboard, and the helicopter began to lift off. Fetterman hastily fastened his seat belt, then took the helmet and ICS cord from the gunner and jammed it onto his head.

"What's up?" he said in an overly loud voice that caused all connected to the ICS to flinch and pull their heads down in a shrug, which again reminded him of turtles.

"One of the log helicopters was making chow drops and reported that one of their patrols didn't show up at the rendezvous point. The patrol hasn't checked in for over two hours now, though there was a brief garbled transmission earlier that sounded like some heavy rock and roll was going on somewhere."

"Not uncommon. Probably got their batteries wet and stopped to let them dry off," Fetterman countered, his breathing evening out and his heart beginning to slow to normal after his muddy sprint.

"That's what I thought, too," the pilot said. "But your feller at A-555 picked up the broken transmission, too. He said there were three words that got out before they were stepped on—*aquila, aquila, aquila*. Say it means something special and that we ought to get up there most ricky-tick and check it out."

Fetterman craned around the corner to poke Willow and get his attention before pulling the helmet to one side and shouting over the engine noise. "What does *aquila* mean?" he asked.

Willow's face blanched slightly, then he leaned forward to bring his lips nearer Fetterman's helmet to speak. "It means *eagle*. It's one of our code words. Means somebody needs a helicopter—fast!"

17

CAMP CARROLL, I CORPS

"I have to admire you boys going back out after what happened with the rope and all," Bates said to his drowsy audience. "I'd have expected no less of either of you, of course, but I want you to know how much it's appreciated. Now, as to what remains to be done."

Gerber sat hunched down in his chair, watching Bates trace his collapsible pointer along the roughly canoe-shaped pattern of map pins that represented the radar reflectors. The canoe would not, however, have been seaworthy, owing to a gap in its stern that represented Co Roc, and this breach was now receiving a thorough going-over with the tip of Bates's pointer. The air was still and sticky inside the operations bunker and reeked of stale cigar smoke that caused Gerber to alternate between periods of nodding and nausea.

"As you can see, a reflector placed near the top of Co Roc, preferably on its southern face, is mandatory to maintain the integrity of our grid. H-hour is...let's see...twelve hours, fourteen minutes from now. Figure sundown at 1900 hours, half an hour for the last light to die, that'll give you two hours to make the drop and get out before the Buffs arrive. Questions?"

Tibbets struggled to a proper sitting position and began clearing his throat; it took several attempts. Gerber noticed that the pilot's eyes looked terrible. They were bloodshot beyond normal with the lids stretched thin over them to the point that he resembled, more than anything, a newborn rodent. His appraisal of Doug made him wonder about his own appearance, but only momentarily, for the air inside the earth-covered metal bunker was as dead and warm as that inside a spare tire and his lungs were beginning to burn.

"Yeah, Colonel . . . sir. I've got a question. My chopper's due for an inspection and will need service on the rotor head before we can fly her again. When do my maintenance boys arrive, and what if we're not up come nightfall?"

"Well, Tibbets, you knew when you came up here that sort of stuff would be limited. I figure you know as much about that machine of yours as anybody around, right?"

"Yes, sir, but—"

"Then I suggest you sky out there a little early and get done what needs doing. Otherwise I think this comes under the heading Operational Necessity, and you'll be forgiven for going a tad over on your scheduled inspections."

Tibbets's mouth hung open for a moment, then slowly closed. The muscles at the angle of his jaw continued to twitch, however, a clear indication to Gerber that Bates's answer had been less than satisfactory. And yet Tibbets remained silent. Then it was Gerber's turn to stare with mouth agape.

"Oh, yes, and you'll be traveling north after you make the drop on Co Roc. The staff decided we really must have at least one NVA from the AO for interrogation," Bates said matter-of-factly. Then, when the men didn't react, he added, "Preferably an officer." There was still no reaction, so he went farther. "A major will do fine, but a colonel would be even better."

Gerber's face filled with blood while his knuckles blanched to an unhealthy ivory shade. Tibbets was still in shock over his maintenance request, but did manage to regain focus once his cohort took the floor.

"Why not Ho Chi-fuckin'-Minh himself, Alan?" he asked. "Why not just go for the main boy? And while we're up anyway, how about we strap General Giap's butt to the skids and he can tell you in person what he's up to? Jee-sus!"

"Now, Mack, don't go getting in a lather. Next you'll be sulking in self-pity with that hangdog look on your face. So we need a little HUMINT from the front—it's not like there's a scarcity of enemy about and I was asking you to go hunting for one. Just cruise along like you've been doing the past few nights, and when you see one separated from the herd, swoop down and nab him!"

"You make it sound so simple, like there's going to be NVA colonels out for solitary strolls, unarmed, incapable of running, just out for their evening constitutionals and amenable to taking a little flight. You *know* it's not like that. It's *never* like that!"

"All right. So I oversimplified it a bit. You know what we need and I know you can get it. So *do*. Any more questions?" Bates hated his words but spoke them with authority, just as the general who had told him had.

Tibbets cleared his throat again. "Where is the major or colonel going to sit? I mean, there's hardly room for the two of us now, what with all the extra gear and all. So where do we put our Charlie?"

"You're the aviation specialist, son. You figure it out. Throw something out if you have to."

As they left the dirt- and sandbag-covered culverts that served as an entrance to the bunker, Tibbets lagged behind to speak with Gerber. The sun was behind angry clouds at the moment, and the air outside seemed positively cool in contrast to that inside. Colonel Bates continued on his way to the base headquarters, leaving the two men gasping and batting their eyes in the light like a pair of frogs in a hailstorm. Once they had adjusted to the light and relieved their seared lungs, they started back to their hootch at a tired pace.

"We were supposed to be home tonight. Do you realize that?" Tibbets said in a whine.

"Never thought I'd hear anyone refer to anyplace over here as *home*, Doug."

"You know what I mean. I'm pooped and so is my chopper. Look here, my ass is dragging my tracks out!"

"You should see your eyes. At least you get the satisfaction of saying 'I told you so' about the prisoner business. How do you recommend we go about that, huh?"

Tibbets brought a hand to the stubble on his chin and massaged it lightly until one particularly stiff whisker speared him, then he turned his newborn rodent eyes on the captain and said, "We don't."

"Meaning?"

"Meaning we don't get the bastard! What can they do, court-martial us? Not unless they want what we've been doing out here made common knowledge they won't. I say we gaff it off."

"We'll see. Maybe one will come handy and I can hog-tie him to the skid or something."

"Whatever you say, Mack, but I'll warn you."

"What?"

"Remember when the colonel said I could 'throw something out' to make room for the gook?"

"Yeah?"

"Well, I'm looking at the only thing that's not bolted down in that cockpit, right now," Tibbets said, eyeing Gerber up and down.

THE HELICOPTERS CARRYING Lieutenant Mildebrandt and his troops were just visible above the horizon to the north as Fetterman's ship began a ladder search of the area where the patrol was last reported. From the relatively safe altitude of three thousand feet the area below appeared peaceful enough, drenched, pocked here and there with bomb craters and speckled with clumps of thick jungle, but peaceful.

Willow continued to transmit his attempts to reestablish radio contact with the patrol but was rewarded with nothing but static and an occasional weak transmission from afar that had ridden the skip two hundred miles or more. At other times there came the nasal roar of another frequency trying to bleed over into his own as the helicopter came into line-of-sight with distant fire bases in the Highlands. After an hour Willow broke off attempts and joined the others at staring out the door in search of the missing patrol.

Once, he spotted fresh tracks along a wide muddy trail, but these belonged to two small boys who were coaxing a pair of water buffalo along. The boys lifted their faces to the sky and waved heartily as the helicopter passed over them, then had to run wide circles around the water buffalo to keep them from bolting in fright. The pilot commented that unattended water buffalo sometimes made irresistible targets for trigger-happy door gunners, so it was only natural that the beasts took the sound of rotor blades as a signal to bolt.

Willow wondered what sort of man would shoot a dumb animal from a helicopter, and with an automatic weapon at that. The thought reminded him of hunting deer back in the mountains of North Carolina and how much ragging he'd taken from his uncles and cousins because he'd declined to shoot a doe he'd tracked down.

The feat had reaffirmed his prowess as one of the best trackers on the reservation, since the deer's trail was over hard, dry ground that was mostly limestone outcroppings—not a soft river bottom where even a rabbit would leave tracks a blind man could follow. Such spoor as there was indicated a large doe moving at an unhurried pace, nibbling at the thickets of honeysuckle vines that covered the treetops left behind when the lumber company had cut through that portion of forest.

Another impression in the dust held his fire, however, a small print that could easily have been made by a falling acorn had the lumber company left an oak large enough to bear acorns. The slight distension of the doe's udder confirmed that she had a fawn hidden somewhere nearby. She was alert, her large ears twitching and the muscles at her flanks rippling as she stood ready to meet whatever threatened her young and to lead that threat away. Willow noisily jacked an unneeded cartridge into his lever-action Winchester 94, and the doe bounded away unscathed. Sam Flint, his uncle, was livid and took great pains to berate him for flushing the deer and even went so far as to compare his heart to that of a white squaw. This, Flint claimed, was why he'd taken his name from his mother, Willow Wind, instead of his father. Flint stopped short of naming Ben's father for the name was unknown to him as it was to Ben, another stigma he had to bear on top of being something less than his family's idea of a man.

"There!" Willow said over the ICS while indicating an area to their north. "They're over there."

"Where?" Fetterman, the Peter Pilot and the command pilot asked simultaneously.

"To the right, about a klick. They're probably in the thick stuff," he said, indicating a dark green crescent of jungle that stood out in contrast to the low foliage surrounding it. A sluggish stream passed nearby, its red water looking like a scalp injury among the stubble of the plain. Willow noted, but didn't mention, that the stream sat deep in its banks and was probably quite old, considering its meager flow. The crescent of jungle probably represented a past bend in the stream that had clogged with vegetation and eventually rerouted itself.

"What makes you think so?" Fetterman asked as he strained to see any motion or sign that might indicate the presence of troops.

"*They* do, Master Sergeant," Willow answered, pointing to a pair of carrion birds that were orbiting the jungle.

LAO HEARD THE HELICOPTER in the distance and quickly moved to the edge of his cover to uncase his binoculars. It took several seconds to locate the aircraft above the horizon due to the sun flooding his lenses but, after sliding back under a low bush in order to shade the binoculars, he saw the helicopter as a mere smudge against the sky. It was orbiting up high, possibly coordinating ground operations, he reasoned, or perhaps searching for their patrol. A flood of other possibilities crossed his mind, many of them ludicrous, as the fever again surged through his body, causing him to shake like a constipated dog. The morphine did nothing for his fever but had relieved the burning sensation on his chest and arrested the rising panic that had caused him to nearly blow the ambush.

Primarily it was the bite wound that had caused it. When the small patrol was spotted, it seemed only too fortuitous. They were visible from a long way off due to the thin vegetation of the area and appeared to be heading for the jungle thicket near the stream, a likely rest spot since it afforded the only true shade for a kilometer or more. He'd arrayed his men along the northern point of the sliver of jungle and waited.

It was a predominantly ARVN patrol with only three Americans, and these were of low rank. The patrol was spread well with point and rear positions covered as they closed on the wooded area, then their discipline broke down. A litter of unburied C-ration cans scattered along the floor of the jungle attested to this being a regular stopping place, and this familiarity no doubt caused the breakdown. The fever was very much upon Lao as he waited to trigger the ambush, waited until the rear guard had joined the rest at the edge of the shade.

He'd briefed his men to hold their fire until he opened up, telling them that this would be as soon as the majority of the enemy had taken off their packs and grounded their weapons, a process that was currently in progress. Some of the South Vietnamese troops had already dropped weapons and packs into a heap and were lighting up cigarettes when he lifted the scope of the Mosin-Nagant to his eye and scanned the enemy. To his delight Lao found the distinctive red cross emblazoned on the pack of one of the Americans, a large black man. The medic swung his pack easily to the ground and dropped his web belt and canteens on top of it. Then he started walking purposefully toward the jungle while wrestling with the fly of his pants.

A magnified sense of urgency flowed over Lao, an unwarranted fear of discovery that caused him to sweep the barrel of his rifle rapidly to find the radioman before the medic walked up on him. The medic, however, was merely seeking the jungle's edge to relieve himself in some degree of privacy and had already stopped well short of Lao's troops.

The radioman, another American, though of what ethnic group Lao couldn't ascertain, was standing apart from the rest and freeing the long whip antenna from its retainer in preparation to transmit when Lao's sight post found him. The rapid swing of the Nagant's barrel took the scope past the radioman and up against a small bush that shuddered loudly under the impact and transmitted its vibrations back down the rifle and into Lao's shoulder and chest. The pain was intense and brought a cry from his lips before he could fight it back. The medic heard this and saw the trembling bush as it slapped noisily at its neighbors.

Without benefit of the scope Lao could see the wide-eyed realization in the man's eye and thought only of silencing him before he warned the others. The Nagant accomplished this in fine fashion, catching the retreating man between the shoulder blades and pushing him forward to slide on his face.

Lao's men squeezed off their first rounds in response to his shot and found their targets immobilized by fear and confusion for that instant it takes even a trained soldier to react. Lao cursed aloud and again sought the radioman in his sights. He found him crouching behind a clump of brush, the long antenna betraying his position. Sliding the cross hairs down along the length of the antenna, he let them come to rest where he reckoned the man's head to be. The Nagant bucked in his arms, and the radioman was thrown from his cover.

A large portion of skull was missing just above the man's jaw, exposing gray-pink brain and an empty eye socket where the bullet had entered. The radio, Lao was gratified to note, hadn't been hit nor had the telephonelike receiver-transmitter, which now fell to the ground as the dead man's hand relaxed its grip. Not all the enemy fell as effortlessly as these two, however.

Looking up from his scope, Lao discovered that the survivors of the first volley were now up and moving. Some merely took to their heels across the open ground, leaving weapon and equipment where they'd deposited them. But others were now defying the basic premise of the ambush and charging into the fray with weapons blazing. A trio of M-16 rounds sang over Lao's head, ticking their way through limbs until striking something substantial.

The RPD opened up, sending a spit of green tracers skipping across the ground toward the oncoming enemy. Two more went down immediately to lie writhing on the soft earth with leg wounds, while a third pulled up suddenly, dropped his weapon and clutched his groin with both hands. A tangle of intestines fell across the man's forearms, yet still he stood clutching himself and screaming his anguish until another volley freed him from pain forever.

A blast of heat against the side of Lao's cheek sent his face burrowing into the soft earth as a grenade exploded in the direction of his machine gunner. The concussion picked Lao off the ground, then slammed him back down hard. The air rushed from his lungs, and steel fingers of pain shot up from his reopened wounds.

The stutter of an M-16 on full automatic, like that of a sewing machine, issued from nearby and sent a score of angry metal wasps zipping through the air. One of the wasps found one of Lao's radiomen and deprived him of a shoulder. The man's screams joined the cacophony briefly until the combination of shock and loss of blood sent him into a coma from which he'd never awaken. An AK-47 barked behind him, and then another as the rear guard added its fire. Hearing this, Lao mistakenly assumed his men were retreating, and again he felt panic begin to pump its ammonia stink into his nostrils.

Lao stood and panned the heavy sniper rifle before him as he took his first steps back toward the heart of the jungle. The trees above and around him danced as bullets slapped against them and sent a hail of bark and leaves cascading down, making visibility through the already smoky underbrush even worse. A heavy crashing sound came from in front of him as someone lumbered through the brush. Lao fired three quick rounds from the hip and stepped back another two paces. A guttural roar followed by a curse in Vietnamese came from the area of the sound, though whether it was an enemy or one of his own, Lao didn't know or care. He took another step back and brought his spine in contact with the trunk of a tree. Spinning, he shot the tree twice.

And then it was over. The firing slowed to single rounds at first, then died altogether until the only sounds were fleeing birds and the moaning of wounded soldiers. Lao barked orders in a voice made shrill by fear and anger and soon accounted for his men. Five were dead, including three around the machine gun, and another six wounded with two of these serious enough to render them nonambulatory.

Lao had to shout at one of his men who was busy putting insurance rounds into the enemy dead. He wanted, needed, in fact, to interrogate any wounded who might remain and deemed himself fortunate indeed to find the last American among these. In short order he had the information he required and then had the enemy bodies hidden in the jungle. He also had another PRC-25 radio, several of the small FM handsets and an M-60 to replace the ruined RPD. And morphine, glorious morphine, along with antiseptic powder for his wounds and aspirin for his fever. It was not, however, enough.

Now, the helicopter continued to circle and was joined by two others. They'd soon land to investigate, he reasoned, and find the ARVN dead along with seven of his own, but they wouldn't find the Americans! Lao was certain of that. At least they wouldn't find them until it was too late. A few booby traps would see to that, and then, as dark approached and most of the helicopters had returned to their base, he'd strike. Satisfied, he gingerly slid back down the steep bank and stooped low to pass under the thick foliage that hung out over the stream. His men averted their eyes as he approached.

They fear me even more now, he thought. The fools! Surely they could see why we couldn't be hampered by the lame, couldn't slow ourselves with litters and risk discovery by keeping the moaning injured with us. The coup de grace, the filthy French had called it, had to be administered to the few for the protection of the many. He was almost certain he'd mentioned that possibility during one or more of their briefings, along with the reasons he absolutely could not allow either himself or any of his men to be taken captive. Another phrase of his adolescent French crossed his mind—*c'est la guerre*—and he saw in the dazed faces of his men that this was so. With a shrug he dropped to a squat and fished a can of rations from one of the captured packs. A faded Polaroid snapshot of an automobile fluttered out along with the rations.

"Fifty-seven Chevy," he read aloud, then smirked at the startled look on the soldier nearest him. He tossed the photograph into the stream and watched it slowly crawl past his ragtag patrol, then he turned the rations can to read its contents. "Peaches!" he exclaimed happily, then thought this must be his lucky day.

As an afterthought he dug out the little packet of four cigarettes that came with each ration pack, provided they weren't stolen at the rear, and tossed it to the soldier. The man fielded the pack in self-defense, then studied it carefully, happy it wasn't a grenade his leader had tossed him. The tension seemed to lift then as the soldiers began investigating their own captured treasures and joked with one another. Lao allowed them to get overly loud, then hushed them with a gentle voice and a smile. He was back in control, and control was everything.

18

THE PLAIN OF REEDS

The lead gunship swooped low on its pass over the sliver of jungle, its guns and rockets at the ready, and found...nothing. The second gunship followed from off a perch, keeping an expectant eye on the first to mark any enemy fire and return same, then, when the lead ship pulled off its run with a negative report, slowed and ran the quarter-moon patch at a crawl. At the end of its run, number two tossed out a white smoke grenade.

"Seems clean, or at least they're being timid," the pilot radioed to the others. "There's a little smoke near my marker and some vegetation tossed around, but no activity that I can see. We're pulling back to the perch and will follow you in."

"Rog," the Peter Pilot said, then looked back over his shoulder to Fetterman. "Y'all ready?"

Fetterman nodded and grabbed the side of his web seat as the helicopter began dropping and gathering speed. From his seat he could see the other two slicks bearing A-555's exec, Lieutenant Mildebrandt, and his men. This, at least, seemed a bit like old times, since he'd worked with Mildebrandt before. The three helicopters descended single file to present the smallest target possible until they were a hundred feet above the jungle canopy, then spread into a fingertip formation for the landing.

The lead ship landed at the northern point of the wooded area while the other two slid off to either side. Troops stepped or jumped from the doors as soon as the ship was near the ground, executed a forward roll, then came up running. In less than a minute all were beneath the shade of the first trees and fanning out to screen the area before them.

"Make damned sure of your targets, people!" Fetterman heard Mildebrandt shout from the opposite side of the forest.

"Over here!" a Vietnamese voice demanded in his native tongue from the north end.

"Slowly!" Fetterman said in a hushed voice to the assistant machine gunner, a new conscript who had started to dash toward the voice. "You can't even be sure that was one of ours, now can you?"

The soldier bowed slightly and shook his head from side to side like a scolded child.

"Never head toward a voice unless you—" the master sergeant began in his most fatherly tone, then was interrupted by a spate of Vietnamese issuing from his FM handset.

"Many dead, many!" the voice said.

Fetterman's skin crawled slightly as his nervous system readjusted itself to put him on an even higher state of alert. Then he keyed his own radio and said, "Watch out for...*booby trap*!"

The assistant machine gunner froze midstep but not before the trip wire rode up his thighs to catch on one of his canteens. He looked as if he were on the verge of falling flat on his back when Fetterman pressed the radio into the man's pack to steady him.

"Just freeze," he said calmly, then gently took the wire next to the soldier's canteen in his hand and squeezed it tight. "Now, you get the wire on the other side and hold it steady. If you feel it give the least bit, get the hell out of here. Got it?"

The man nodded and took the wire across his waist into one trembling hand while lowering his rifle to the ground with the other. When his weapon fell safely at his feet, he took the free hand and lifted his canteen ever so slowly. Sweat was standing out on his face and beginning to drip from the tip of his nose by the time the wire slipped free and he fought off an inclination to turn and run. He rolled his eyes in their sockets as though to ask Fetterman, "What do I do next?"

"Hold the wire steady now. Take this side, too, and just hold it there. Could be the type that triggers on release or delays. Willow?"

"Here, Sarge!" came the voice at his elbow.

Fetterman hated being called Sarge, detested it, in fact, but at the moment his central nervous system didn't have room for annoyance. "You trace it toward the clearing. I'll take it back this way. Sing out when you find something."

The pair separated to follow the taut wire to its origins, a painfully slow process due to the care that had to be taken to clear each step to avoid other booby traps. Fetterman was almost certain there would be others; why else would this one have its trips strung so high off the ground? Obviously the enemy expected them to find it, wanted them to probably, and would lay other, more discreet traps to be hit while avoiding the blatant one.

Fetterman's end of the wire ran for fifteen meters, then terminated in a knot around a sapling. This, he thought, is what saved us: the sapling was small and limber enough to give before tripping the mine or grenade at the other end. He waited a full five minutes for Willow to announce finding the device and, when Willow had remained silent, started back. His brows furrowed when he saw Willow standing a short distance past the sweating machine gunner with hands on hips looking his way.

"Well?"

"Well, what? Did you disarm it already?" Willow asked in return.

"I found the anchor!" Fetterman shot back.

Willow smiled, then reached out and jerked the trip wire out of the machine gunner's hands. It sang a bass hum as it went tight, a fitting accompaniment to the acrobatics the machine gunner and master sergeant were performing as they scrambled to put the thick tree trunks between themselves and the obviously demented Indian. Willow's smile blossomed into a deep laugh, and the sound carried through the surrounding forest.

"Come on out, Master Sergeant. I found an anchor, too!"

"You *what*?"

"I said, there's an anchor on my end, too. It's just a wire strung between two points to slow us down, that's all."

"It'll do it, too. Damn! Don't ever pull any shit like that again, Willow, or I'll..." Fetterman left the sentence unfinished while he tried to think of something appropriate.

"Sorry 'bout that. Just couldn't resist."

"Next time, do. Now, let's get up ahead and see what they've found. You'll need to get on the horn and tell our boys up there we'll need some Dust-offs, then we'll see if you're as good a tracker as you are a prankster."

Scarcely a klick away Lao listened intently as Willow passed along the mission request, paying particular attention to the extraction codes and comparing them to those he'd tortured out of the wounded American before he'd died. The changes were subtle, but noted, despite the fact that the first of the transmission was curiously garbled.

19

CAMP A-555

"Looks like he did it to us again, huh?" Maxwell admitted mournfully.

Stonehand pulled one side of his headset forward to rest against his cheek, the better to hear the red-faced CIA man while still monitoring the radios.

"Maybe. At least we know he hasn't gone back north yet."

"Christ! I'm not so sure that's anything to be happy about the way things are going. How many dead this time?"

"All the ARVNs, for sure. Still haven't located the U.S. advisers, but Fetterman reports a blood trail into the jungle that he's following. The going's slow, though, due to booby traps. That makes an ideal setup for another ambush if you ask me."

"How about support?"

"Two Dust-offs are on their way to take out the dead and another is standing by in case they get jumped or we find the advisers. No problem there, but the Crusaders need to break it off in a couple of hours. There are some infantry troops in the field who need gunship support, too. The Hornets say they'll stay with us as long as we need them, which stands to reason since their guys got stung by this dude."

"And the Provider?"

"Preflighted and ready with a crew on standby. Five minutes notice they can be airborne and on the scene within another fifteen. The pilot has done Fulton extractions before. One here and two in the States."

"Lucky to have him. Has he done any at night?"

"Has anyone?"

"Good question. You say he's done one over here?" Maxwell tipped the last can of Coke in A-555 to his lips and allowed a tiny sip to enter his mouth. He let the warm liquid sit on his tongue, relishing its effervescence and salivating until it was diluted, then swallowed. "Seems I remember an operation a couple of years ago, now that you mention it, but it wasn't in-country, was it?"

"Not technically, no. A Colt observation plane was brought down along the Trail by some LRRPs, a lucky shot that apparently got the pilot 'cause the aircraft continued for a ways into Cambodia before crashing. A comm station picked up a Mayday call about the same time, and it was in *Russian*."

"I see. So naturally G-2 wanted the pilot's body for propaganda, right?"

"Right. I was with the A-team that parachuted in to get him and, believe me, most of us were pissed that the Commie was to get a ride home while we were left to walk back across Stormy Weather. Anyway, we found the wreckage and the pilot and sent him out by Fulton."

"What did he look like?"

"Stew meat. No papers, no insignia, no propaganda. Just a splattered Soviet with a magnetic compass sticking out of his forehead and about five zillion flies."

"Maybe we'll have better luck this time, eh? If the boys don't find something soon, I think we should pull them back in for the night. Don't care much for the idea of holing up here while most of the troops are gone."

"Getting nervous? Minh's still here, and he knows his stuff pretty well, I understand," Stonehand said.

"I know, and I *should* trust him. I know that, too. But I keep remembering that this very camp fell once before, and it was an inside job at that. I just think we'd all feel better if we circled the wagons here before nightfall and started again at dawn, that's all."

"What a colorful experience, 'circle the wagons.' Not much of a tactic if you really think about it."

"Served the pioneers pretty well against...well, you know."

"Did it now? I understand our Plains brothers really appreciated it because it enabled them to ride around at full tilt without having to stop and reverse course. Whatever. Seems the military likes the idea still. Reckon they've got the wagons circled up at Khe Sanh?"

"I'll be sure and check on that when I get back. Anything interesting comes over the wire, let me know," Maxwell said, then slid off his stool and marched up the steps from the communications bunker and out into the fading sunlight.

Maxwell remained in the interior of the compound, roaming from the team shack out around the fire control tower and then back to the team shack again. Each time he entered the shack he paced over to the purring refrigerator and peered inside, hoping against hope that somehow another Coke had materialized there. At last he resigned himself to the fact that there would be no more and settled for a beer. He was still scrubbing the rust marks off the top of the beer can when Galvin Bocker straight-armed his way through the door with an announcement.

"Word just in. They've found the American advisers, all of them."

"Alive?"

"Not even close. Stonehand took the call from Fetterman's RTO, and it was all in Cherokee. Seems the bodies were hidden carefully, and Tony thinks our boy may have wanted us to think they'd made it out."

"Maybe. If this was even Lao's work."

"Not much doubt about that. The ARVN bodies were pretty carved up, but he took extra pains with the Americans. One of them may have even been alive for a while, they say, 'cause his skin was hanging in ribbons from his ribs and he'd bled nearly dry."

"Sounds like Lao, all right. Okay, ask Fetterman if he's got any idea which way Lao went back and then get them back into the choppers. Chances are our siren has pulled back across the border by now but, just in case . . ." Maxwell considered his words, smiled at them, then spoke them. "Tell Stonehand to have them circle the wagons."

"HOW'D YOU THINK to look up there?" T.J. Washington asked.

"It's the way you track. First you picture the area as perfect then look for imperfections. The vines up there are pretty thinly scattered except in those forks where they covered the bodies," he lied, then decided to square with the medic. "Actually I was looking at the ground, like the rest of you, when I found this puddle of blood over here. While I was looking for splatters coming in or going out from it, a drop fell right in the middle of the puddle, so I just looked up."

"Wonder why in hell they put 'em way up there?"

"To slow us down, same as all the trip wires. It worked, too, didn't it?"

"I reckon it did. I'd better tag and bag these boys. Damn, they do look rough, don't they?"

"That they do," Willow agreed softly, unable to take his eyes off the mutilated corpses that now stared at him with lidless eyes and grinned hideously from lipless mouths.

Kit stood to one side, staring at the bodies and feeling hot tears of shame well up in her eyes. No wonder Americans thought her people were barbarians, she thought. No, she corrected herself, Lao could not be said to be *her* people any more than the rest. Her kind were held apart from society due to their mixed parentage, a difference that had alternately been a source of pride and prejudice. Lao, she decided, could not even be considered human—he was an animal, a rabid wild thing whose mind had become poisoned. For a rabid wild thing there was only one cure, and she hoped to be the one to administer it.

"We're going to ex-fil back into the choppers as soon as Dust-off gets here for these, Kit, and I'm thinking of sending one of them back to base for a while. Do you want to go on it?" Fetterman asked after noting the pained look on her face.

"No. You will need me to identify Lao, correct? If you still want to take him prisoner, that is," she said firmly.

"Our orders are still the same, though I'll admit I'm beginning to wonder why," he said, partially understanding Maxwell's contention that, if the VC really did kill Lao's parents, he might be tempted to cross over, and partially hoping circumstances would rule out that option and commit this maniac to the death he so richly deserved.

"I think we both know why, Sergeant Tony. Who would know better than myself, eh?"

Fetterman considered the fact that Kit had also been on the other side not too long ago, a bona fide Co Cong, but couldn't begin to see similarities between her and Lao. She hadn't ambushed and massacred U.S. troops, for one thing, or *had* she? She was still an enigma to him, an unknown quantity.

"By the way," she uttered while looking up at him and crossing her arms as though she were cold, "thank you for believing in me. I . . . I needed that very much."

"We all do at times, I suppose. When we get back you can buy me a drink, if you like, and we'll call it square. I just ask that there be no more surprises, that's all. If you're Uncle Ho's favorite niece or anything like that, let's hear it now, okay?"

Kit smiled, arched her back catlike and stretched. Then she covered her mouth with one small hand to hide a yawn. The smile returned as a sparkle in her eyes as she said, "Well, I wouldn't say I was his *favorite*, but . . ."

Fetterman was almost certain she was kidding, almost. Kit's eyes darted to one side, causing him to follow her gaze. Willow was approaching at a trot.

"Hornet Six was just on the horn. They're getting a weak UHF transmission that could be our boy! He's asking for a Medevac and using these guys' call sign, authentication and extraction codes. And get this, you know the personal questionnaires the SAR boys keep on file for no-code extractions?"

Fetterman nodded, remembering his own and how it had come in handy once when he'd been "detained" for a few days by the VC.

"Well, Lao must have really done his homework 'cause he even knew what model car one of these guys owned!"

"CONFIRM YOUR PRIORITY as immediate. Are you still in contact with enemy, over?"

"Negative, negative. Cold LZ, I repeat, cold LZ. Say time en route, over," Lao transmitted in what he felt was an excited enough voice.

"Wait one," came the reply.

In the helicopter the Peter Pilot was having a hard time believing he was actually conversing with an NVA officer, while his pilot silently cursed at the spinning needle of his ADF. To make matters worse the carrier wave of Willow's SSB kept interfering as he worked through two TACPs en route to the DASC. His efforts, while irritating, were fruitful, and a pair of A-7s heading toward Vinh Long were diverted to them. Hasty conversations between the cockpit and Willow provided estimated wind direction, elevation of target, run-in headings and a catalog of other information to be passed on.

All of this was based on speculation since as yet they hadn't managed to lock up Lao's transmitter and fix his position. Further discussions of who would serve as FAC—one of the Hornets—and how the target would be marked followed. Fetterman suggested they let Lao mark the target for them and call it just prior to their run, and that Willow make damned sure the bombers knew they weren't to hit the target directly but to straddle it.

"I'm working on getting you a chopper from the nearest unit and maybe save some time. Could you give me your co-ordinates again and spell out the grids phonetically this time, over," the Peter Pilot transmitted after a time.

Lao hesitated, rolled onto his back to measure the sun's progress across the sky and felt the handle of his new knife dig into his spine. He sat up and jerked the miscreant blade from its scabbard and started to toss it into the sluggish stream. It was a bayonet and, as such, somewhat longer than the knife the scabbard was designed to carry. His other knife, however, was the appropriate size, so he swapped them and found the arrangement much more comfortable. His finger traced imaginary lines across the map from his position out to the corresponding grid identification letters at the side and top margins, then extrapolated his numeric plot within the grid square identified. He spoke deliberately, trying to keep exasperation from his voice.

The pilot gave a vigorous thumbs-up just prior to the end of Lao's transmission, a signal that he had an ADF lock on Lao's receiver. Two of the other units also locked on his transmission with the resultant lines of position that fixed his position.

"Roger, copy. Dust-off estimates your posit in zero-plus-two-zero mikes. Confirm you have smoke, over."

"Affirmative, we have smoke. Understand twenty minutes. Quebec Three-Two out," Lao replied, allowing a heartfelt tone of relief to flow through the handset. Then to his soldiers he said, "Twenty minutes! Everyone, get in positions and remember—wait until the ship lands and shoot to kill. No prisoners this time. Just take all medical supplies and whatever weapons you want, then put a grenade in the helicopter and come back here. Comrades, we're going home!"

20

CAMP CARROLL, I CORPS

Damned if you do, damned if you don't, Doug Tibbets thought as he wiped at an oily fuel stain with a rag. You don't top off the tank and it sweats, adding water to your fuel. You do top it off and the heat of the day expands the fuel until it leaks all over the place, like now. He walked over to a covered trash can marked Combustibles and deposited the sodden rag, then stood and looked back at the Quiet One. What he saw didn't inspire confidence. The bubble was filthy, rather like trying to look through a gin bottle really, and the hodgepodge of junk stuffed into the tiny cargo area behind the seats lent a Fibber McGee's Closet appearance that cluttered the ship's normally clean lines. Still, he had to admit, it beat walking. Anything, no, *everything* beat walking over here! Given the choice between fight and flight, he invariably saw flight as the viable alternative.

Not that he felt himself a coward. Far from it. Not many cowards volunteered for duty in Vietnam flying gunships, and even fewer went through test pilot school, but the brief moments of exposure afforded a speedy aircraft seemed preferable to prolonged hours and days of paranoia on the ground. To his mind the two modes of combat were like entering the water for the first time in late spring. You can dunk a toe into it, then a foot, wade out to knee depth and then sit, or you can step up to the bank and commit yourself to a belly buster and be done with it. His first tour in gunships was like that—hours of boredom spiced here and there with moments of stark terror. But it still beat walking.

His footfalls echoed off the walls of the temporary hangar as he walked back to the helicopter and started cleaning the thin Plexiglas bubble. The grime was mostly JP-4 from all the time spend at a hover the past three days. No, not days, *nights*, he corrected himself. Besides the oily smoke residue there was a diverse collection of insects splattered across the nose, but the film of JP-4 kept them from sticking tightly.

Idly, Tibbets considered that one could tell at what altitude an aircraft had been operating just by what species of insect accumulated on its nose. It stood to reason that grasshoppers would rarely be encountered at three thousand feet, and the same went for beetles. Not so with bees and butterflies, though. They could be anywhere, like birds. Rule of thumb on bird strikes in the Army: if you hit a buzzard, and survived it, you were okay, but hit a chicken in flight and you're back to walking again.

The approaching night had an uncharacteristic chill to it. That made it all the better to hover, he reasoned, but, just the same, he took the precaution to toss out all but three of the reflectors. The packets of small cones remained and gave him cause to question the diversity of things called into service in the name of war. It was almost a parody, a sick statement there somewhere, but he couldn't quite fight through the cobwebs of fatigue to put it into words. In the end it all came down to the same yardstick: if it works, what the hell?

He was about to consider whether the soldier back at MACV HQ would get his promotion as promised for the idea when a rattle at the canvas door announced the arrival of his partner. Partner in crime? a mental sprite asked. Yes, he concluded, if you get right down to the short and curlies, it probably is a crime of some magnitude. At least it would be in the press, and that's where this war was really being fought—and lost.

"She ready to go?" Gerber asked, stifling a yawn.

"At least as ready as we are, I'd say. You stop by the mess tent and get coffee?"

"Yes, and no. I stopped, but there wasn't any coffee made. Sergeant Woodard was at the back of the tent reading and didn't seem the least bit inclined to make any. Downright surly, now that I think of it. Must have something on his mind."

"What was he reading?"

"A paperback. Catchy title, though—*Soul on Ice*."

"Hmm. Never heard of it. Probably a crotch novel about Eskimos or something. I make it about an hour till dark, so what say we find some doggies to drag this bitch outside."

"Everything all right? I mean, you expressed some concern at the briefing."

"It'll do. Just a little tired, that's all. A lot like ourselves, huh?"

"Yeah. I'm beginning to wonder how vampires do it."

"Maybe that's why there are so few of them in-country, Mack, and I have a feeling all those are staff pogues."

"Ah, well, let's get out there and get it over with," Gerber said in a resigned voice.

Tibbets nodded and set out in search of a ground crew, wondering each step of the way if the captain's *it* referred to the mission or life in general.

"ROGER. KEEP SHARP, Ben. Don't go counting *coup* on us now!" Stonehand said into his microphone, then leaned back in his chair.

"So they're inbound to the LZ, huh?" Bocker asked from his position on the stool.

"Affirm. They should be in place within five mikes and have their ambush set in another five. The Dust-off is staying with them to cover their tracks."

"How's that?" Maxwell asked from his seat at the end of the radio panel, his red face neutralized in the crimson glow from the radio lights so that he seemed pale.

"The VC are like birds, see? If you want to catch a bird, you send two or three people into a thicket. Birds can see well enough, but they can't count. So when a person or two comes back out, the bird figures they're all gone. This is the same thing. Charlie, or in this case Lao, can hear helicopters, but he can't tell how many. So when the master sergeant's ship drops down to infil them, no one will be the wiser."

"Clever," the CIA man said. "Does it work?"

"Most of the time," Bocker answered. "What was the stuff about counting . . . something?"

"Counting *coup*. It's an Indian thing. You white folks didn't import combat to North America, you know. We had our campaigns long before y'all showed up. You just brought better technology to streamline the affair, that's all. Anyway, our fights weren't the all-out mess wars have come to be. It might just be to settle a dispute over a hunting or fishing territory, hardly worth massacres and pitched battles that would cost many lives. Instead, we'd just have a battle at a reduced level. Oh, there'd still be a few folks take an arrow or a spear, but the braves that emerged from the battle as heros—as true men—were those that actually touched an enemy with his bare hands. This was called counting *coup*, and only the first one or two to do it received credit. Among some tribes it was a required rite of passage into manhood."

"Why only one or two per battle?" Bocker asked, beating Maxwell to the punch.

"Because otherwise the battle would be reduced to a game of touchy-feely, for Christ's sake! Couldn't have two noble tribes out pawing around on one another, now could we? But now that you mention it, the fact that only a few could count *coup* in each battle was probably an incentive to have battles on a regular basis. Wonder what rationale our Great White Chiefs are using nowadays?"

"The Mighty Green Buck, most likely," Maxwell opined, then hushed as the radio crackled to life.

THE DUST-OFF SHIP stayed a few hundred feet up while the slick dropped down to just above the stubble and scrub of the plain. At a point less than a klick behind Lao's position, the chopper flared and then flattened to a hover while its soldiers piled out. Fetterman was the last to leave, having to wait until the others were in place before tossing down the Fulton. Owing to the length of time since its last inspection, he didn't want to take the chance of it landing hard and rupturing the cylinder of helium.

The Dust-off completed its orbit overhead as the slick rose to join it briefly before breaking off and retiring to the south to wait. For Fetterman's troops the waiting was almost over and the thought of the three American bodies in the Dust-off made their efforts seem all the more urgent.

The handful of soldiers started forward at a low trot until well clear of the area where the helicopter had landed, then fanned out as briefed. Washington and Willow stayed back with Fetterman as two of the principal players while Kit took a position nearby. Krung and Kepler melted into the brush and headed toward the more substantial vegetation that lined the stream ahead.

Once out of sight of the rest, each sought a thick bush to which he tied the anchor end of trip wires and began reeling out the wire as they spread apart. Every fifty meters or so a booby trap was attached to the wire, usually a simple affair consisting of a grenade with its pin pulled stuffed into a C ration can to keep the actuating spoon pressed down. A tug on the wire would pull the grenade free and, three seconds later send a spray of hot metal flying through the air.

The last two traps on either side, however, were claymores and from these the men ran a veritable octopus of trips back and forth between them to better insure their being sprung. The operation took less than the allotted five minutes but left the pair winded and soaked by the time they rejoined the others to take up their positions. Fetterman made a brief tour of the area and, satisfied with the placement of his meager forces, signaled for Willow to relay their readiness. Willow depressed the transmit button on his URC-10 twice, holding it down for a three-count each time.

Sergeant Krung plucked a handful of thick grass from behind him and stuck it between his back and his pack, then snatched another handful and pushed it down the back of his collar to break up the lines of his helmet. The grass was brittle and scratched his skin, but that only served to help him stay alert. He was feeling the usual anticipation he felt prior to action, a sort of low hum in his ears as adrenaline started to gather for its rush. The real rush would come once the enemy was in his sights, and it would peak just prior to his pulling the trigger.

With each initial squeeze he pushed aside the thought that his target could well be some poor farmer who really had no heart for fighting but was pressed into service by the hated Vietcong. He pushed these thoughts out by substituting a memory of his village in ruins, his family lying murdered amid the bodies of his neighbors and friends, his sister raped. She later killed herself because her honor was gone. Revenge would add its bitter poison to the adrenaline to give him the singleness of purpose to concentrate on killing the enemy and to harden his heart to their screams, as his family's murderers must have ignored their screams, and to take from each a token of his manhood—the manhood.

But today it was different. The oath he'd sworn over his family's graves was so close to being realized, yet the American master sergeant had ordered him not to take trophies from his kills. Where, then, was the incentive to kill? Where was the feeling of justice that would grant him his vengeance and purge his soul of its thirst for it? And why, of all the enemy they'd faced together, did Fetterman choose this particular one to deny him? He felt something worse than the adrenaline and hate; he felt futility and he felt betrayed.

"QUEBEC THREE-TWO, this is Dust-off Three-Seven, over."

Lao heard the transmission as though from afar, a morphine-and fever-induced haze in his head vying for control. He pressed the transmit button only to have his sweaty thumb slip off it before he could speak. He shook his head to clear it, then spoke aloud before depressing the button to measure his voice, and to make certain he was speaking English.

"Quebec Three-Two, go ahead," he said through dry lips.

"Roger. We're near your position now. Can you hear us, over?"

Lao sat up and lifted a wide frond from in front of his face and strained to hear over the gurgle of the stream, which seemed to get louder the more he tried to eliminate it from his mind. A muffled thumping sound came from the east.

"Roger, I hold you due east of my position."

"Good! Pop me some smoke to gauge my winds and we'll have you scarfed in a heartbeat. Understand three wounded, affirmative?"

"Affirmative," Lao answered, then subconsciously held the handset to his chest as he yelled for his men to toss a smoke grenade into the clearing.

"I see purple. Confirm purple?"

"Roger, purple," Lao said, aware of the sound of the helicopter getting louder as it closed the distance between them, along with a keen whining noise just at the limit of his hearing range. This he put down to an aberration of his fever.

The smoke grenade sent up a plume of purple that rose uniformly until it was above the shelter of the trees, then caught a light breeze and flattened out until it formed a hazy L standing on its head. The sun was almost behind the horizon now, sending long shadows from the tree line out onto the muddy plain and making it impossible for the pilot to discern the presence of soldiers between the smoke and the woods. He continued his high-speed run toward the smoke, hoping the element of surprise worked equally well on both sides. One hundred meters short of the smoke where he would normally begin his flare and deceleration maneuver, he lifted the nose of the helicopter slightly and pressed the microphone trigger switch on his cyclic stick.

"Everybody ready?" he asked.

Two short clicks in his headset came as his answer.

"By the way, what are you guys selling today?"

"Grunts, four each," the flight lead said calmly.

"Hot damn!"

THE MACHINE GUNNER WAS TENSED, ready. Through the purple haze the helicopter continued to grow larger and louder until its throbbing, thumping blades matched the rhythm of his own heart. The red cross on the ship's nose was discernible now; how foolish of the Americans to give them such a distinct aiming point! Now the nose was lifting in preparation to stand on its tail and stop its run before settling to the ground . . . but, no!

To the gunner's consternation the helicopter continued to go up until it slipped out of sight directly overhead. Perhaps it was coming in too fast, he thought, and would circle and come back. His eyes returned to the open field in time to register a pair of gray streaks coming toward him. With horror he recognized the oblong shapes that fell tumbling through the air beneath each aircraft as they pulled up into a screaming, climbing turn to set up for a strafing run.

Lao saw the helicopter pass overhead, still climbing straight into the setting sun, and wondered. Wonder turned into gut-wrenching panic as the BLU-27 napalm bombs sent a wall of fire leaping and snapping into the air on either side of him. Even over the roar of the departing jet engines he could hear his men crashing and thrashing their way toward him in full retreat. The temptation to shoot the first ones he saw washed over him as the first choking wave of smoke drifted into his nostrils. No, he thought, as frightened as they are they'd likely fire back! Better to remain under the protective lip of the creek bank until friend and foe alike had left the field, then make his way across the three klicks of plain to the border and take his chances on the medication there.

The first of his men went splashing past, some with weapons, others without, to scale the red dirt of the opposite bank and continue their flight. Run, you fools, run, he thought, then his attention was drawn to a new sound upstream. The surface of the slow-moving stream was alive with floating napalm, a movable wall of fire which withered and burned everything alongside the banks as it crept downstream. The baritone growl of the jets' 20 mm Gatling guns came from behind him followed by the detonation of a small bomb forward and to his left. There was no choice—he could either face the same fate as his men or stay here and surely burn.

Lao leaned back to shake the radio free from his shoulders and, in his haste, managed to reopen several of his wounds. The blood was cold against his sweaty skin and the pain only moderate over the morphine. With detached interest he noted the widening dark stain on the front of his shirt, then gauged the advance of the fiery stream. The jets returned for another strafing pass, though none of their rounds made it even as far as the stream, and Lao chose the occasion of their pull-off to hurry across and up the bank.

His advance was rapid through the thin scrub of the plain, and the welcome edge of the triple-canopied jungle that was the Cambodian border loomed but a few kilometers ahead. At near full speed he ran from bush to bush in an attempt to keep himself hidden from the marauding jets, occasionally craning his head back over his shoulder to watch for their advance. During one scan behind him his foot became fouled, and he pitched facedown onto the soft earth only to be lifted upward by the explosion he'd triggered. His hands clutched at clumps of grass to hold himself to the earth as the air above him filled with flying steel balls. He diverted his course away from the explosion and continued to run.

KIT LAY INVISIBLE beneath the boughs of a low shrub and mentally measured the enemy's advance by watching the geysers of fire-tinted dirt that rose from each booby trap. Now she could make out their heads above the brush, could hear them crashing through it like spooked oxen. The first one was inside the perimeter now, now past Krung's position, now even with her own and heading full tilt toward the tree behind her. They held their fire. Even through the veil of years she knew from her brief glimpse that neither of these first men was Lao and, since they were unarmed, she let them pass.

Two others followed close behind, one of these limping and sporting a dirty bandage that had slid from high on his leg down to around his ankle. Neither of these two was Lao, either, so she left their fates in the hands of the others as two additional heads bobbed into view and then a third. Shots rang out behind her as the fleeing men ran into the ambush, and yet the men ahead of her continued forward as though deafened in their desire to gain the sanctuary of the border. The first of the lead pair stopped short and offered to lift a rifle to his shoulder, but her own barked first and he no longer had an eye to aim with. Krung cut the legs from beneath the other with a well-placed shot to the knee. The third man disappeared into the brush just as yet another appeared behind him.

The fire was sweeping the plain now, the two walls started by the napalm joining near the stream and consuming the dry grass and stubble as it came toward them with the light breeze. The smoke rose in a white sheet and rained a constant confetti of ash and cinder that threatened to spread the fire even farther. In the distance a grenade exploded, sending a tall shower of earth and ash into the sky to hang there for an instant before obeying the pull of gravity and crashing back to the scorched earth. A spate of green tracers bounded along the ground toward where Fetterman and the rest lay hidden.

Krung raised the barrel of his M-79 and fired, seeking to lob a grenade behind the stalled enemy and coax them forward. The launcher uttered a tenor *bloop* and sent its projectile into the air halfheartedly, like the last shot from a Roman candle. The snub-nosed grenade landed between Lao and the man firing the tracer ammo, exploding with a force that belied its small size. The soldier was lifted high into the air with a severed arm whirling away from him like an obscene boomerang. Lao was flung backward by the blast to land hard on his back. He arched upward and slid a hand under him to the small of his back, fully expecting to find his spine exposed. Instead he found the hilt of the knife, which had only scraped him. Relief at finding himself intact gave way to darkness as a welcome unconsciousness claimed him.

21

THE PLAIN OF REEDS
SUNDOWN

'Over here, T.J.!" Fetterman shouted.

The medic low-crawled the ten meters with an M-16 in the crooks of his elbows. Random shots still interrupted the constant crackle and roar of the brushfire, but it was just insurance rounds going into clumps of brush that might yet hold an enemy—an enemy just like the one Washington encountered on his crawl, although probably one who hadn't had his kidney vented by a razor-sharp Case VS-21, as this one had. The man stared at him as he slithered by to join Fetterman, who was crouched behind a bush that was already beginning to smolder.

"Willow caught one in the throat, T.J. Can you do anything?" the master sergeant asked, knowing the answer only too well.

"Let me see," Washington offered, then knelt beside the fallen man and lifted his head with a gentleness rare among big men. "Through and through the jugular, and not enough left to resection. Nothing I can do here 'cept maybe pray."

"Damn. Well, let's drag him away from here a piece anyway. Fire's spreading pretty fast and we'll have to *di di* soon."

"I'll take care of this. You go ahead with the rest," Washington offered, then lifted Willow by his armpits and started to drag him easily back along the path he'd just crawled.

Had Washington been less intent on scanning the area for enemy he might have seen Willow's hand reach out as they passed the enemy soldier and touch the man on the shoulder. He might even have seen the expression on the young Indian's face change from a grimace of pain into something akin to peace as his eyes dimmed and his heart stopped pumping. Instead he saw that he'd left the URC-10 where Willow had fallen and that it was about to be claimed by the flames. Washington sprinted to the radio, slung it over his shoulder and slowed his pace as he headed forward to join the rest. High overhead, a specially configured C-123 Provider droned through the azure sky occasionally catching a flash of fading sun on its windshield.

The dead who had fallen at the fringes of the ambush were in danger of being caught up in the fire, so they were inspected first. Nothing on these soldiers was found to set them apart from others of their ilk, and Fetterman was about to despair of finding their main quarry until Kit shouted his name and waved from a position near the middle of the field. He walked rapidly over to her, mindful of their own booby traps and trip wires, and immediately spotted the dismembered soldier at her feet. The man appeared to have been about her age, though the current state of his remains made this a rough estimation. He was about to ask when she walked off toward the forward most point of contact. Then he saw the other body and went to join her.

Lao was back in a familiar dream, complete with voices and smells. The spring odor of the new fields as they were slashed and burned for the year's row crops came to his nostrils along with the overripe stench of newly turned earth. There was another smell that didn't belong to the dream, an acrid, pungent odor like a spent fireworks shell. But the voices, they fit. They were talking about him, saying his name. He knew one

of the voices and the recognition roused him from his half sleep
and brought his eyes down to focus through the swollen slits
that were his lids. It *was* her! The hand beneath him instinctively sought to clench into a fist of rage but was prevented
from doing so by the hilt of his knife.

"You're sure it's him?" Fetterman asked.

"It's Lao, as I said," Kit replied, the huskiness of her voice
revealing her loathing.

"I'll get Washington over here to check him out, but from
the looks of that chest I'd say he's a goner," he said, then
turned to wave the medic forward.

Kit stepped forward to look down on Lao and to feel all the
old hatred rise as a bitter bile in her mouth, as if to coax her
into doing what she wanted to do anyway. She stared down at
the slits of eyes and blood-darkened chest of the man who'd
treated her so cruelly then pursed her lips and let go a stream
of spittle that landed in a splat across his forehead. Fetterman
heard this and turned in time to see Lao arch his back and slash
out and up with his knife. The impact of his thrust lifted Kit
off her feet and sent her sprawling. She attempted to crawl on
her back away from her attacker. Lao struggled to his feet, the
knife clutched tightly in his blood-drenched hand as an ani-
mal-like growl escaped from his throat.

Fetterman started to lift his rifle, to aim low for the legs, but
found Kit's head backing into his sights. He lowered the rifle
and watched in horror as Lao gained his feet, made three un-
certain steps toward Kit, then stopped with his knife raised
high over his head. Fetterman raised his weapon again, cen-
tered it on Lao's chest and fired. Lao spun out of his sights
before the firing pin went home and the staccato crack of an
M-16 a short distance from his ear sent Fetterman's shot wide.
Lao now lay writhing in pain alternately clutching his shoulder and his chest. Fetterman looked around to find Krung
standing to one side behind him, the still-smoking barrel of
his weapon tracing small circles in the air as he continued to
track his target.

"No, Krung! See that he has no more weapons. T.J.? Kit's hurt!"

Kit sat in a growing pool of blood, clutching her thigh and rocking back and forth slowly, her eyes fixed upon Lao and a thin smile parting her lips. Washington widened the slash in her fatigue pants and recoiled from what he saw. The knife had entered at midthigh and dug in deeply. Now jets of arterial blood sprayed upward with every beat of her heart.

"He nicked the femoral artery. We got to get her the hell out of here and back to a MASH, *now!*" Washington announced.

Kit seemed not involved at all and neither resisted nor assisted when Washington finished ripping the leg from her fatigues and applied a tourniquet as high above the wound as he could reach. She seemed content to sit and die while watching her nemesis do the same. Washington hesitantly checked Lao while Krung kept his M-16 pressed tight against the NVA's neck.

"How about him?" Fetterman asked after Washington had torn away Lao's shirt and inspected his wounds.

"About the same. Nothing but bad ones today. He's losing a lot of blood from the shoulder wound, and I removed a piece of rib that was sticking out of his side. Damnedest thing! That rib belonged to that guy over yonder. Grenades do funny things, huh? Don't guess I'll ever get used to that sort of thing. Oh, yeah, and the chest wounds are old. Looks like he got into a scrap with some sort of animal. They're all infected and loaded with pseudomonas. I'd say he needs to be evacuated right away, too."

"Any other wounded?"

"Got another VC over there with his knee blown off. He's in shock and fading fast. None of our folks have 'fessed up to wounds, 'cept for Willow of course."

"All right. You and Krung keep an eye on our wounded, and I'll see if I can get them a lift out of here."

Fetterman's first try on the SSB was successful, the Provider requesting local wind conditions and elevation, then citing the gathering darkness as cause for hurry. His efforts with the Dust-off ship, however, were less fruitful. He was certain his transmissions were going out but paused to inspect the URC-10 anyway. It was intact and functioning, but still he could get no reply from the helicopters and was beginning to fear they'd run low on fuel and returned to base. He tried his hand-held FM unit and received an answer, of sorts. A voice came back in Cherokee and, though he spoke none of the language himself, he understood it to mean "No Cherokee, no response," just as briefed.

The sun glinted off the C-123 as it banked to make a dry pass over the area, causing Fetterman to pull back his helmet and run a hand through his thinning black hair and wonder at the situations man routinely put himself in and the decisions that had to be made. That, he reasoned, was the reason the military gave orders—to serve as a framework for decision-making—and as he himself was fond of saying, orders were orders.

The balloon rose slowly into the dark purple sky, a bubble of pale yellow hope that tugged its cable stubbornly upward until it caught the last light of day and turned a deep, glowing gold. Fetterman rechecked the harness, still concerned about its age but realizing that time, not age, was the governing factor now.

The big twin-engined aircraft rolled out of its turn and flattened its approach. It looked like a particularly ungainly moth with the lacy Y-shaped feelers on its nose. It aligned itself with the smoke to run into the wind and reduce its ground speed, then made small jinking corrections until the balloon fit between its sights. The men scrambled away to clear a departure path for the harnessed passenger, then watched slack-jawed as the aircraft engaged the cable. The harness held and tugged its passenger off the ground far more gently than any of the men had imagined. The aircraft went into a gentle climb, and before it was out of sight the lump trailing below and behind it had merged with the open rear door. The men on the ground cheered, all but one.

"Now wasn't that slick!" Kepler shouted happily.

Fetterman smiled into the darkness himself until brought back to the situation at hand by a comment from Washington.

"Now, what are we going to do with Lao? He ain't gonna last much longer."

Fetterman looked around at the expectant faces, each reflecting the glow of the brushfire and each looking anxious to be on their way.

"Major Lao perished in the ambush and was consumed by this fire, as best I recall," Fetterman said, hardly believing the words were his own.

"Yeah, I seem to remember that," Washington said.

"Me, too," Kepler agreed. "And it couldn't have happened to a nicer guy, neither!"

"Okay, so what should we do with the *late* Major Lao until he becomes sure enough late?" Washington asked.

"I think I'll leave Sergeant Krung in charge of him while we retire to a more defensible position and wait for the boys in that Provider to send us a slick. How about you two carrying Willow and I'll square everything with Krung."

The master sergeant approached the Nung tribesman and spoke to him.

"Why do you tempt me, Sergeant Tony?" Krung asked. "You know I hate this man, and I know you do, too. He will die from my bullet soon enough. Why not—"

"Sergeant Krung, do you remember our conversation about your, uh, collection?"

"Yes, of course I do."

"You will recall that I ordered you not to take trophies from your kills' dead bodies. Is that correct?"

"Yes, it is so."

"*Dead* bodies, *dead*. I distinctly recall forbidding you from touching *dead* bodies, Sergeant Krung. We're going to work our way around the fire to a pickup spot on the creek bank right through there. You join us after Major Lao and the other one have departed life. Remember to call out before approaching our position, and I'll expect you there within fifteen minutes.''

Krung smiled his understanding and nodded. To Lao, who understood the words if not their meaning, the smile bore a simple terror that was as paralyzing as it was just.

22

CO ROC, LAOS

The blanket of mist that routinely cloaked the valleys in that section of Laos was very much in evidence as the Quiet One crawled across the landscape and up the southern approach to Co Roc. The sky overhead was a boiling black cauldron that threatened to release its drenching load of rain at any second, and the winds swirled and gusted up, down and around the mountain. From the opposite side occasional flashes signaled outgoing 152 mm and long-range 130 mm shells due to fall on the sequestered Marines on Hill 881S and the rest. The fiery tail of a 122 mm rocket crossed the sky in the distance, adding its deadly six-foot warhead to the destruction. In all it painted a picture of a type of war Gerber hadn't experienced, and didn't long to.

The winds buffeted the little helicopter, rocking it from side to side as it sought each new current like a hooked fish trying to spit out a lure. Yet up the hill they climbed, unnoticed by the enemy and unknown to the Marines in Khe Sanh and the B-52 crews that had already lifted off from their fields in far-away Guam. At a point three-fourths the way up, Tibbets eased back on his cyclic and lowered the collective a fraction of an inch, bringing the ship to a halt in midair.

"This looks like about it, Mack," he said in a hushed voice. "Any higher and I won't have enough power to hover with you hanging under me. She's not putting out like I thought she would and this density altitude is rough enough without the winds."

"Whatever you say. Maybe if we dropped a little lower it would be easier," Gerber suggested while rechecking his harness and ropes.

"I'd like to, but then I wouldn't have a horizon to work with. You don't want to see what trying to hover on instruments looks like. I'd be popping your ropes like a buggy whip."

"You're right, I don't want to see that. Okay, here goes."

Gerber stepped out into the downblast and leaned back against the cockpit to pull his weight against the ropes and test their attachment one last time before lowering himself over the side. Knowing this was to be the final rappel reduced the soreness in his arms and shoulders and made the descent easier. The fog boiled about him as he entered the bowl-shaped dimple in the fog bank caused by the helicopter's downwash, and soon everything disappeared. It was like being inside a cave without a light, a thick, saturated darkness so all-encompassing that senses of balance and sight were soon lost. After what seemed an eternity, his feet brushed against something solid. A snag, he thought, then felt the surface crumble under him as he lowered himself another six inches.

Ground? The realization shot through him that he'd dropped through the trees all the way to the surface of Co Roc in the fog. Momentarily relieved of his weight, the helicopter started to rise, pulling his ropes taut and lifting him back into the air. In the cockpit Tibbets fought to control the copter as it bobbed over its changing load, then settled again into its soft purr, interrupted occasionally when a miscreant wind came around the mountain to slap playfully at the spinning blades. Tibbets noted with mounting alarm that his oil temperature was slowly creeping up to the top of the green arc on its gauge and again wondered if he should have grounded the helicopter until proper maintenance could have been performed. Another tug from below sent his mind and eyes back to the horizon as he concentrated on holding his position.

The helicopter wandered slightly to one side—Gerber was at a loss to know which side since he was again inside the blinding cloak of fog—and brought the ropes up against the outer branches of a tree. Birds sleeping in its boughs fled on thrashing wings, causing Gerber to flinch and start himself spinning. With his free hand he reached out and waited until leaves and stems filled his palm, then clamped down. His gyrations halted, he used one leg to keep in constant contact with the foliage while pulling himself back up the rope until the branches began to slope away from him at the treetop.

He kicked out to bury a foot in the thick branches, then used this hold to pull himself close. Gerber locked off the ropes and brought the reflector out with a flourish. With a flick of his wrist he deployed the umbrella and sank its shaft into the tree limbs until it sat like an overturned bowl on the surface of the world's largest salad bar. Halfway back up he felt the rain of shiny cones pass him in the cloud and wished the local monkeys *bon appétit*.

"Are we done?" Tibbets asked after Gerber had regained the cockpit and donned helmet, goggles and seat harness.

"With that part, anyway. You know, you could have waited until I was back before dropping your goodies."

"Did I hit you?" the pilot asked, his grin pinkish through the night vision goggles.

"Close enough. Now, what say we climb up and watch the war while I catch my breath?"

"I was about to suggest the same thing myself. We need to get some airflow over our oil cooler anyway. I was beginning to think I was going to have to leave you for a while."

"Over my dead body!" Gerber exclaimed, feigning outrage.

"Probably. Care for a tour of the valley?"

"I was thinking more about what's on top, actually. Of course I could have just walked on up there while I was on the ground, I suppose."

"On...the...*ground*?"

"Yeah. Somehow we managed to miss the whole forest, but I won't tell if you don't."

"Deal. Jesus, no wonder this old gal was bucking and jumping back there. Our man on Co Roc! Quite a distinction being the lone American walking around up there. Make a great war story one day."

"Yeah, but I'd have to have you along to back me up. I doubt anyone would ever believe most of this operation anyway. In fact, I have a hard time dealing with it myself."

"I think that's the whole idea. It's so farfetched that no one, least of all the VC, are looking for it. Maybe your colonel has his head screwed on straight after all. Hang on."

The plunge down the side of the mountain sent Gerber's inner ears to swelling until he managed to hold his nose and blow to equalize the pressure. When they were halfway around Co Roc's northern face, it lit up under a barrage of artillery fire, clearly delineating the layers of cloud above and fog below. Near the apex a particularly long tongue of flame licked into the sky only to disappear into nothingness, even through the goggles. While on their next circuit the position at the peak again spewed flame but, unlike the other heavy weapons that were at least discernible under camouflage nets, it melted into the hillside like a memory. This phantom weapon intrigued both men, along with the obvious destructive power it represented.

"You want to take a look?" Tibbets asked, not sure he really wanted an answer.

"Might as well. I figure we take a look up there and maybe bring some intel back that'll smooth the G-2's feathers if we don't get a volunteer NVA to take home."

"Then we're not going Charlie hunting after all?"

"I didn't say that. I was just wondering if we had enough fuel to do that after it took so-o-o-o-o long to get the reflector in place, that's all."

"I see what you mean. Well, let's go then."

The helicopter seemed to sense its trials were nearly at an end as well, for it climbed eagerly to altitude and skimmed the surface of the mountain as if it had an aerie at the peak. Near the tree line at the top Tibbets left the mountainside and pulled his craft away to rise above and orbit the peak. Gerber strained through his goggles to keep focused on the dark patch where he reasoned the artillery battery to be but saw nothing, not even the usual clump of netting, for several moments. Then a long barrel came out of the side of the mountain, raised to a high angle and belched flames as it sent its load of death and destruction toward Khe Sanh. When the flames and smoke had cleared, there was again nothing.

"It's a cave!" Tibbets declared. "A friggin' gun in a cave!"

"Shades of World War II, huh?" Gerber agreed.

"I think we should definitely phone this one in."

"Not yet. How are you at pinnacle landings in this thing?"

"You don't mean . . . up there? Do you?" the pilot asked.

"Up there" identified itself with another tongue of flame, then lapsed back into darkness.

"Why not? If we get close and see the troops on the ground, we'll just bug out and be done with it. If not, I'd like to hop out and see if I can't derail the damn thing. If it's not too heavily defended, I ought to be able to get a grenade or two in there and mess up their aiming ring if nothing else."

"And you expect me to wait for you, right?"

"That would be nice."

They circled the peak, nudging up against the low clouds, and scanned its surface for enemy, seeing none.

"Can't believe they don't at least have a spotter up here," Tibbets said.

"May be too chilly for him. Besides, they have the cave site and should have every target pretty well zeroed in by this time. Let's go down."

"I want to go on record as thinking this is a dumb idea, Mack, and if you fiddle-fart around down there, don't be surprised if I don't stick around!"

"Five minutes, Doug, then hightail your butt out of here. But leave me some of that high-energy stuff, if you have any left. It'll be a long walk back to civilization."

The helicopter kissed the stone surface with its skids and settled onto the flattened peak, a feature that caused Co Roc to remind Gerber of a rifle projectile when viewed from afar. Tibbets overrode his basic instinct to keep the ship at flight rpms and rolled off the throttle to ground range. The blade flattened and became even quieter. Gerber grabbed his AK-47 and started for the edge at a trot, paused to look down the slope, then disappeared over the side.

From the slick path leading down he knew the peak was used regularly as an observation post or fire control spotter, which made its uninhabited state seem all the more suspect. Then he saw the volume of rounds being poured into the clouds from the batteries below and reasoned that an all-hands effort was underway.

The path forked a short way down to lead off to the northern face. Gerber followed the path along a narrow ledge that hugged the mountain like a goat trail. The long muzzle of the 130 mm peeked out of the cave's mouth, lifted itself to the night and then roared. The concussion of the blast sent a cascade of small stones over the edge and along the path to join others strewn there and caused Gerber to sit back against the mountain's face abruptly. When he looked again the gun was gone. He left the path and climbed higher to approach the cave from slightly above.

Even in the chill of night most of the soldiers attending the weapon were stripped to the waist and glistening with sweat. He watched while four men rolled the heavy weapon forward on its tracks while three others fought a round into its breach and locked it home. When the gun reached the end of its rail, one of the loaders cranked the elevation handle to raise the barrel under the watchful eye of an officer who then stepped gingerly forward to pull the lanyard. The gun rolled backward on its tracks from its own recoil, its barrel lowering automatically and the whole works disappearing into the mountainside. On either side of the cave's mouth sat antiaircraft emplacements, a precaution Gerber considered overkill given the difficulty of the target. He peeled back the strap from his watch and noted that two of his allotted five minutes had elapsed.

Gerber slid on the seat of his pants into position beside the mouth and waited for the gun to make its way back out. Again he counted the soldiers in attendance and chanced a peek into the interior to see if there were others. The inside of the cave was lit by two gas-powered lanterns and was as much shadow as substance, telling him little. As the nose of the barrel cleared the cave, he pulled the pins from two grenades, taking care to let the rings on the pins slide down his thumbs and not fall to the ground. Something Tibbets had said about artillerymen's hearing told him it was an unneeded precaution, but he held tightly to them anyway. As the steel wheels clanked up against their stops, he released the spoons, waited until they had flipped clear, then rolled the grenades across the rock floor toward the gun.

The first grenade skittered up against the near track and bounced back two feet to sit spinning on the floor. The second lodged beneath the heavy undercarriage. They detonated together with a deafening blast that rivaled the 130 mm's and was amplified by the cave. Gerber fought to maintain his grip on the wall as shrapnel flew past him to rattle its way up the ledge, then he dropped to a crouch beside the cave's mouth with his AK-47 panning the floor inside.

The four pushers and one of the loaders had caught the brunt of the first grenade and lay motionless with flecks of blood covering their naked torsos where shrapnel had entered directly from the blast or ricocheted off cannon and cave walls. The second grenade had lifted the big gun up at the rear and left it poised over the brink, its breach hanging open and almost touching the roof of the cave. The other two loaders were hit by the blast from beneath the gun and now half sat, half lay on the floor with most of their lower legs missing.

The officer had been shielded from the shrapnel by his position behind the gun, the others having already jumped clear of its recoil-powered trip back inside, but he lay motionless, too, thin streams of blood trickling from nose, mouth and ears from the concussion. Gerber again peered into the depths of the cave and again saw no one. At a crouch he crossed the floor to the NVA officer's side and checked the pulse at the man's throat. He was still alive. He pat-searched the man for weapons and came up with a revolver and two grenades. The former he tossed over the side and the latter he placed on the floor nearby.

Tossing the unconscious enemy across his shoulder, he hurried to the path and paused to deposit the man alongside the mouth of the cave where his two grenade pins still lay. Back inside the cave, Gerber pulled one of the dead soldiers up next to the caisson and pushed the two grenades, without their pins, beneath his body, hoping that when the enemy got around to investigating, someone would dislodge the grenades and complete the job of pushing the 130 mm over the side.

The artillery volley from below continued apace as Gerber arrived beside the helicopter. Tibbets was shouting incoherently out the door the whole time he was securing his rappeling ropes to the enemy's ankles, and the rpms were gaining rapidly by the time he sprang into the cockpit and donned his helmet.

"... get us both killed in the process, by God!"

"I'm sorry, Doug," Gerber said as the ship began to lighten on its skids and fight its way up into the thin air. "I missed most of that."

"I said I can't see this bird lifting whoever that is and us, too. Especially not at this altitude! Are you crazy?"

"Just following orders, Doug," Gerber answered, though he wondered if maybe he might be crazy, just a little. Then he pulled the Ironmonger blade from his shoulder strap and flourished it before Tibbets, admiring the craftsmanship. "That's why he's on a leash! We have any trouble, I just reach out and snip him free. Any problems with that?"

"You're beginning to sound just like your colonel, you know that?" Tibbets mumbled, then dipped the nose of the craft forward to run out over the edge and fall to cruising speed.

A shrill scream came from behind them as they departed. Gerber correctly assessed it as the NVA officer regaining consciousness. The man's head hung down from his tether, spinning around with eyes and mouth open wide. Tibbets remembered to shed their static electricity buildup by keying his FM mike before landing, lest he barbecue the gook's heart on contact with the ground. Then he called ahead for a cargo receiving crew to relieve them of their "sling load." They were finally on their way back to Camp Carroll.

A little later, as they walked from the flight line to their hootch, Tibbets asked, "What rank was that guy, anyway?"

Gerber ran a hand across his stubbly jaw and thought. "I didn't notice—an officer anyway. Probably a lieutenant. Why?

"Well, I seem to recall Bates putting in an order for a major or better, and one that was headed north at that. This guy wasn't headed *anywhere*!"

"Yes, he was. We're north of Co Roc, aren't we? He just didn't know he was headed north at the time. A minor technicality, Doug. You worry too much, you know that?"

In the southwest a false sunrise painted the jagged horizon as, six miles up, radar navigations in the bowels of eight B-52s released their loads of over a hundred five-hundred-pound bombs each. Casualties in the "canoe" were high; an NVA captured later admitted that one of General Giap's retreating regiments had lost three of every four men in the air strike.

EPILOGUE

MACV HEADQUARTERS
SAIGON

Gerber stepped from the tailgate of the Chinook and onto the blistering tarmac of Hotel Three to stand shielding his eyes from a sun far brighter than the one he remembered. Nearby, a jeep waited for him, its driver nodding behind the chained steering wheel. The drowsy driver stirred when Gerber tossed his bag behind his seat and walked around to slide in on the passenger side. New sergeant stripes clung precariously to the faded sleeves of the driver's fatigue shirt.

"Sergeant, now, eh?" Gerber asked.

"Yes, sir!"

"Are those stuck on with Jiffy-Sew, by any chance? If so, you might want to get them out to a *mamasan* and have them sewn on right, or they'll peel off in a few days."

"Well, you see, sir, if everything goes right, I might just have to replace them with some staff sergeant's stripes in a week or two!"

"Well, well, making the grade kinda quick, aren't you?"

"Yes, sir. In fact, I just might re-up if this keeps happening."

"Good idea," Gerber said while fishing around in a side pocket of his fatigues. "Care for one of these?"

The sergeant looked at the silver cones in the captain's hand and smiled broadly.

"As a matter of fact, sir, they've become my favorite."

Tony Fetterman sat in the shade outside the headquarters building, waiting. His debrief was a simple affair—don't say anything about anything to anybody—and wasn't it a pity that, after all they'd gone through, Lao had managed to walk straight into a booby trap and die. Now it was his captain's turn and, though he hadn't known it immediately, Bates could have just as easily borrowed Maxwell's script.

An MP at the main door raised a hand in salute and stepped aside to let Gerber pass back out into the sun where he stood blinking for several seconds before recognizing his master sergeant. "Tony! How was your vacation?"

"Fine, Mack. Nothing like getting back to the old homestead and a couple of nice walks in the country to refresh a fellow. Yourself?"

"Can't complain. A little mountain air, a few nights out."

"That bad, huh? It shows, too."

"You're no daisy yourself. Want to join me over at the Carasel? I'll buy the steaks and you can buy the beer."

Fetterman considered how to phrase his refusal without having to break his oath of silence so close to where it had been given. "No, thanks. I have to go visit a lady in the hospital. By the way, here's your letter."

Gerber took the pastel envelope reluctantly, verified the Seattle postmark, then walked over to a nearby trash can and dropped it in. Then he fished the last of the silver cones from his pocket and offered them to Fetterman.

"Here. Give your lady a kiss for me," he said.

"Hershey's Kisses? I didn't think you even liked chocolate, let alone the kind that's apt to melt all over your pockets."

"Oh, I'd say they're experiencing something of a major peak in popularity over here just now. In man and beast alike. Catch you later, Master Sergeant."

"Yes, sir," Fetterman said with a salute, then marched over to the trash can and tossed the soft candies in with the letter before starting off to the hospital.

GLOSSARY

AC—Aircraft commander. The pilot in charge of the aircraft.

ADO—A-Detachment's area of operations.

AFVN—Armed Forces radio and television network in Vietnam. Army PFC Pat Sajak was probably the most memorable of AFVN's DJs with his loud and long "GOOOOOOOOOOOOOOD MORNing, Vietnam!" The spinning Wheel of Fortune gives no clue about his whereabouts today.

AK-47—Assault rifle normally used by the North Vietnamese and the Vietcong.

AO—Area of Operations.

AO DAI—Long dresslike garment, split up the sides and worn over pants.

AP ROUNDS—Armor-piercing ammunition.

APU—Auxiliary Power Unit. An outside source of power used to start aircraft engines.

ARC LIGHT—Term used for a B-52 bombing mission. It was also known as heavy arty.

ARVN—Army of the Republic of Vietnam. A South Vietnamese soldier. Also known as Marvin Arvin.

ASA—Army Security Agency.

AST—Control officer between the men in isolation and the outside world. He is responsible for taking care of all the problems.

AUTOVON—Army phone system that allows soldiers on one base to call another base, bypassing the civilian phone system.

BISCUIT—C-rations.

BODY COUNT—Number of enemy killed, wounded or captured during an operation. Used by Saigon and Washington as a means of measuring progress of the war.

BOOM BOOM—Term used by Vietnamese prostitutes to sell their product.

BOONDOGGLE—Any military operation that hasn't been completely thought out. An operation that is ridiculous.

BOONIE HAT—Soft cap worn by a grunt in the field when not wearing his steel pot.

BUSHMASTER—Jungle warfare expert or soldier skilled in jungle navigation. Also a large deadly snake not common to Vietnam but mighty tasty.

C AND C—Command and Control aircraft that circled overhead to direct the combined air and ground operations.

CAO BOI—A cowboy. Refers to the criminals of Saigon who rode motorcycles.

CARIBOU—Cargo transport plane.

CHINOOK—Army Aviation twin-engine helicopter. A CH-47. Also known as a shit hook.

CHOCK—Refers to the number of the aircraft in the flight. Chock Three is the third, Chock Six is the sixth.

CLAYMORE—Antipersonnel mine that fires seven hundred and fifty steel balls with a lethal range of fifty meters.

CLOSE AIR SUPPORT—Use of airplanes and helicopters to fire on enemy units near friendlies.

CO CONG—Female Vietcong.

COLT—Soviet-built small transport plane. The NATO code name for Soviet and Warsaw Pact transports all begin with the letter *C*.

CONEX—Steel container about ten feet high, ten feet deep and ten feet long used to haul equipment and supplies.

DAC CONG—Sappers who attacked in the front ranks to blow up the wire so that the infantry could assault an enemy camp.

DAI UY—Vietnamese army rank equivalent to captain.

DEROS—Date Estimated Return from Overseas Service.

DIRNSA—Director, National Security Agency.

E AND E—Escape and Evasion.

FEET WET—Term used by pilots to describe flight over water.

FIRECRACKER—Special artillery shell that explodes into a number of small bomblets to detonate later. It is the artillery version of the cluster bomb and was a secret weapon employed tactically for the first time at Khe Sanh.

FIVE—Radio call sign for the executive officer of a unit.

FNG—Fucking New Guy.

FOB—Forward Operating Base.

FOX MIKE—FM radio.

FREEDOM BIRD—Name given to any aircraft that took troops out of Vietnam. Usually referred to the commercial jet flights that took men back to the World.

GARAND—M-1 rifle that was replaced by the M-14. Issued to the Vietnamese early in the war.

GO-TO-HELL-RAG—Towel or any large cloth worn around the neck by grunts.

GRAIL—NATO name for the shoulder-fired SA-7 surface-to-air missile.

GUARD THE RADIO—Term that means standing by in the commo bunker and listening for messages.

GUIDELINE—NATO name for the SA-2 surface-to-air missiles.

GUNSHIP—Armed helicopter or cargo plane that carries weapons instead of cargo.

HE—High-explosive ammunition.

HOOTCH—Almost any shelter, from temporary to long-term.

HORN—Term that referred to a specific kind of radio operations that used satellites to rebroadcast messages.

HORSE—See *Biscuit*.

HOTEL THREE—Helicopter landing area at Saigon's Tan Son Nhut Airport.

HUEY—UH-1 helicopter.

ICS—Official name of the intercom system in an aircraft.

IN-COUNTRY—Term used to refer to American troops operating in South Vietnam. They were all in-country.

INTELLIGENCE—Any information about enemy operations. It can include troop movements, weapons capabilities, biographies of enemy commanders and general information about terrain features. It is any information that would be useful in planning a mission.

KA-BAR—Type of military combat knife.

KIA—Killed In Action. (Since the U.S. wasn't engaged in a declared war, the use of the term KIA wasn't authorized. KIA came to mean enemy dead. Americans were KHA or Killed in Hostile Action.)

KLICK—Thousand meters. A kilometer.

LIMA LIMA—Land line. Refers to telephone communications between two points on the ground.

LLDB—Luc Luong Dac Biet. The South Vietnamese Special Forces. Sometimes referred to as the Look Long, Duck Back.

LSA—Lubricant used by soldiers on their weapons to ensure they would continue to operate properly.

LP—Listening Post. A position outside the perimeter manned by a couple of people to give advance warning of enemy activity.

LZ—Landing Zone.

M-3A1—Also known as a Grease Gun. A .45-caliber submachine gun that was favored in World War II by the GIs. Its slow rate of fire meant the barrel didn't rise. As well, the user didn't burn through his ammo as fast as he did with some of his other weapons.

M-14—Standard rifle of the U.S., eventually replaced by the M-16. It fires the standard 7.62 mm NATO round.

M-16—Became the standard infantry weapon of the Vietnam War. It fires 5.56 mm ammunition.

M-79—Short-barreled, shoulder-fired weapon that fires a 40 mm grenade. These can be high explosives, white phosphorus or canister.

M-113—Numerical designation of an armored personnel carrier.

MACV—Military Assistance Command, Vietnam, replaced MAAG in 1964.

MAD MINUTE—Specified time on a base camp when the men in the bunkers would clear their weapons. It came to mean the random firing of all the camp's weapons just as fast as everyone could shoot.

MATCU—Marine Air Traffic Control Unit.

MEDEVAC—Also called the Dust-off. A helicopter used to take wounded to medical facilities.

MIA—Missing In Action.

MONOPOLY MONEY—Term used by servicemen in Vietnam to describe the MPC handed out in lieu of regular U.S. currency.

MOS—Military Occupation Speciality—a job description.

MPC—Military Payment Certificates. The Monopoly money used instead of real cash.

NCO—A noncommissioned officer. A noncom. A sergeant.

NCOIC—NCO In Charge. The senior NCO in a unit, detachment or a patrol.

NDB—Nondirectional Beacon. A radio beacon that can be used for homing.

NEXT—The man who said it was his turn to be rotated home. See *Short*.

NINETEEN—Average age of combat soldier in Vietnam, as opposed to twenty-six in World War II.

NOUC-MAM—Foul-smelling sauce used by Vietnamese.

NVA—North Vietnamese Army. Also used to designate a soldier from North Vietnam.

ONTOS—Marine weapon that consists of six 106 mm recoilless rifles mounted on a tracked vehicle.

P(PIASTER)—Basic monetary unit in South Vietnam worth slightly less than a penny.

PETA-PRIME—Tarlike substance that melted in the heat of the day to become a sticky black nightmare that clung to boots, clothes and equipment. It was used to hold down the dust during the dry season.

PETER PILOT—Copilot in a helicopter.

PLF—Parachute Landing Fall. The roll used by parachutists on landing.

POW—Prisoner Of War.

PRC-10—Portable radio.

PRC-25—Lighter portable radio that replaced the PRC-10.

PULL PITCH—Term used by helicopter pilots that means they are going to take off.

PUNJI STAKE—Sharpened bamboo hidden to penetrate the foot. Sometimes dipped in feces.

PUZZLE PALACE—Term referring to the Pentagon. It was called the Puzzle Palace because no one knew what was going on in it. The Puzzle Palace East referred to MACV or USARV Headquarters in Saigon.

REDLEGS—Term that refers to artillerymen. It comes from the old Army where the artillerymen wore red stripes on the legs of their uniforms.

REMF—Rear Echelon Motherfucker.

RINGKNOCKER—Graduate of a military academy. The term refers to the ring worn by all graduates.

RON—Remain Over Night. Term used by flight crews to indicate a flight that would last longer than a day.

RPD—Soviet 7.62 mm light machine gun.

RTO—Radio Telephone Operator. The radioman of a unit.

RUFF-PUFFS—Term applied to the RF-PFs—Regional Forces and Popular Forces. Militia drawn from the local population.

S-3—Company-level operations officer. Same as the G-3 on a general's staff.

SA-2—Surface-to-air-missile fired from a fixed site. It is a radar-guided missile nearly thirty-five feet long.

SA-7—Surface-to-air missile that is shoulder-fired and has infrared homing.

SACSA—Special Assistant for Counterinsurgency and Special Activities.

SAFE—Selected Area For Evasion. It doesn't mean that the area is safe from the enemy, only that the terrain, location or local population make the area a good place for escape and evasion.

SAM TWO—Refers to the SA-2 Guideline.

SAR—Search And Rescue. SAR forces would be the people involved in search-and-rescue missions.

SECDEF—Secretary of Defense.

SHORT-TIME—GI term for a quickie.

SHORT-TIMER—Person who had been in Vietnam for nearly a year and who would be rotated back to the World soon. When the DEROS (Date of Estimated Return from Overseas Service) was the shortest in the unit, the person was said to be next.

SINGLE-DIGIT MIDGET—Soldier with fewer than ten days left in-country.

SIX—Radio call sign for the unit commander.

SKS—Soviet-made carbine.

SMG—Submachine gun.

SOI—Signal Operating Instructions. The booklet that contained the call signs and radio frequencies of the units in Vietnam.

SOP—Standard Operating Procedure.

SPIKE TEAM—Special Forces team made up for a direct-action mission.

STEEL POT—Standard U.S. Army helmet. The steel pot was the outer metal cover.

TAOR—Tactical Area of Operational Responsibility.

TEAM UNIFORM OR COMPANY UNIFORM—UHF radio frequency on which the team or the company communicates. Frequencies were changed periodically in an attempt to confuse the enemy.

THE WORLD—The United States.

THREE—Radio call sign of the operations officer.

THREE CORPS—Military area around Saigon. Vietnam was divided into four corps areas.

TOC—Tactical Operations Center.

TO&E—Table of Organization and Equipment. A detailed listing of all the men and equipment assigned to a unit.

TOT—Time Over Target. Refers to the time the aircraft is supposed to be over the drop zone with the parachutists, or the target if the plane is a bomber.

TRICK CHIEF—NCOIC for a shift.

TRIPLE A—Antiaircraft Artillery or AAA. This is anything used to shoot at airplanes and helicopters.

TWO—Radio call sign of the intelligence officer.

TWO-OH-ONE (201) FILE—Military records file that listed all of a soldier's qualifications, training, experience and abilities. It was passed from unit to unit so that the new commander would have some idea about the capabilities of an incoming soldier.

UMZ—Ultramilitarized Zone. The name GIs gave to the DMZ (Demilitarized Zone).

UNIFORM—Refers to the UHF radio. Company Uniform would be the frequency assigned to that company.

USARV—United States Army, Vietnam.

VC—Vietcong, called Victor Charlie (phonetic alphabet) or just Charlie.

VIETCONG—Contraction of Vietnam Cong San (Vietnam-ese Communist).

VIETCONG SAN—Vietnamese Communists. A term in use since 1956.

WHITE MICE—Referred to the South Vietnamese military police because they all wore white helmets.

WIA—Wounded In Action.

WILLIE PETE—WP, white phosphorus, called smoke rounds. Also used as anitpersonnel weapons.

WSO—Weapons System Officer. The name given to the man who rode in the back seat of a Phantom; he was respon-sible for the weapons systems.

XO—Executive officer of a unit.

ZAP—To ding, pop caps or shoot. To kill.

THE *BARRABAS SERIES*

**The toughest men
for the dirtiest wars**

JACK HILD

*"...a wealth of detail...
gripping... (Nile Barrabas)
does the job!"*
—**West Coast Review of Books**

Nile Barrabas was the last American soldier out of Vietnam
and the first man into a new kind of action. His warriors,
called the Soldiers of Barrabas, have one very simple am-
bition: to do what the Marines can't or won't do. Join the
Barrabas blitz! Each book hits new heights—this is brawl-
ing at its best!

Available wherever paperbacks are sold.   SOBS-1B

**GOLD
EAGLE** ®

**The struggle continues
in a land of death . . .**

JAMES AXLER
DEATH
LANDS.
Ice and Fire

A startling discovery that will alter the lives of Ryan Cawdor and
his band of postholocaust survivors is made when the group finds
several cryogenically preserved bodies and encounters rene-
gade bikers who call themselves ''Hell's Angels.''

Available in December at your favorite retail outlet, or reserve your copy for November shipping by sending your name, address, zip or postal code along with a check or money order
for $4.70 (includes 75¢ for postage and handling) payable to Gold Eagle Books:

In the U.S.	In Canada
Gold Eagle Books	Gold Eagle Books
901 Fuhrmann Blvd.	P.O. Box 609
Box 1325	Fort Erie, Ontario
Buffalo, NY 14269-1325	L2A 5X3

Please specify book title with your order.

GOLD
EAGLE

DL-8

DON PENDLETON's
MACK BOLAN ®

More SuperBolan bestseller action! Longer than the monthly series, SuperBolans feature Mack in more intricate, action-packed plots— more of a good thing

			Quantity
SUDDEN DEATH finds Bolan unknowingly programmed to assassinate the President of the United States.	$3.95	☐
ROGUE FORCE pits Bolan against the very men who trained him.	$3.95	☐
TROPIC HEAT is an adventure about politics and organized crime.	$3.95	☐
FIRE IN THE SKY forces Bolan to confront a fanatical group of the Pentagon's elite who are preparing the ultimate weapon.	$3.95	☐
ANVIL OF HELL follows Bolan across the Sudanese Sahara in an effort to thwart the plan of a powerful consortium to attack the Middle East.	$3.95	☐

Total Amount $ _____
Plus 75¢ Postage   .75
Payment enclosed _____

Please send a check or money order payable to Gold Eagle Books.

In the U.S.A.	In Canada	SMB-1AR
Gold Eagle Books	Gold Eagle Books	
901 Fuhrmann Blvd.	P.O. Box 609	
Box 1325	Fort Erie, Ontario	
Buffalo, NY 14269-1325	L2A 5X3	

GOLD EAGLE ®

Please Print

Name: _____

Address: _____

City: _____

State/Prov: _____

Zip/Postal Code: _____

A stark account of one of the Vietnam War's most controversial defense actions.

VIETNAM: GROUND ZERO™

Shifting FIRES

ERIC HELM

For seventy-seven days and nights six thousand Marines held the remote plateau of Khe Sanh without adequate supplies or ammunition. As General Giap's twenty thousand troops move in to bring the NVA one step closer to victory, an American Special Forces squad makes a perilous jump into the mountainous Khe Sanh territory in a desperate attempt to locate and destroy Giap's command station.

Available in January at your favorite retail outlet, or reserve your copy for December shipping by sending your name, address, zip or postal code along with a check or money order for $4.70 (includes 75¢ for postage and handling) payable to Gold Eagle Books:

In the U.S.	In Canada
Gold Eagle Books	Gold Eagle Books
901 Fuhrmann Blvd.	P.O. Box 609
Box 1325	Fort Erie, Ontario
Buffalo, NY 14269-1325	L2A 5X3

Please specify book title with your order.

SV-2

Take 4 explosive books plus a mystery bonus FREE

Mail to **Gold Eagle Reader Service**®

In the U.S.
P.O. Box 1394
Buffalo, N.Y. 14240-1394

In Canada
P.O. Box 609
Fort Erie, Ont. L2A 5X3

YEAH!   Rush me 4 free Gold Eagle novels and my free mystery bonus. Then send me 6 brand-new novels every other month as they come off the presses. Bill me at the low price of just $14.94— an 11% saving off the retail price - plus 95¢ postage and handling per shipment. There is no minimum number of books I must buy. I can always return a shipment and cancel at any time. Even if I never buy another book from Gold Eagle, the 4 free novels and the mystery bonus are mine to keep forever.

166 BPM BP8S

Name
(PLEASE PRINT)

Address
Apt. No.

City
State/Prov.
Zip/Postal Code

Signature (If under 18, parent or guardian must sign)

This offer is limited to one order per household and not valid to present subscribers. Price is subject to change.

4E-SUB-1DR